GALLOWS HILL

GALLOWS HILL

by Rory O'Brien

The Merry Blacksmith Press

2014

Gallows Hill

© 2014 Rory O'Brien

For information, address:

The Merry Blacksmith Press
70 Lenox Ave.
West Warwick, RI 02893

merryblacksmith.com

Published in the USA by The Merry Blacksmith Press

ISBN—0-61596-619-5
978-0-61596-619-9

In Memory of Ed Hill

*One of the kindest, most generous people
I have ever met.*

Miss you, big man.

NOTE:

While this book is set in a real city, I have taken some liberties with the location and its denizens (though fewer than you'd probably think). I hope my readers and the citizens of Salem will indulge me when I have chosen creative license over strict accuracy; no offense i' th' world.

Chapter I

PEERING THROUGH A BLURRY RAIN, Detective Andrew Lennox made out the shape of the corpse hanging from a gnarled tree at the foot of Gallows Hill.

Lennox often wondered if the tourists and the pilgrims who came in search of legend-haunted Gallows Hill were disappointed or merely puzzled to find it here in a city park, hidden away in a quiet neighborhood of vinyl siding and above-ground pools and crowned by a hulking water tank. It was the kind of trick Salem liked to play on visitors. Aside from the giant witch-on-a-broom silhouette painted on the tank, it was like any other park in any other quaint New England town. It was empty today, abandoned under the soaking rain that had poured down all night long. Two police cruisers were parked in the grass along with an ambulance, lights flashing, yellow crime scene tape stretched between them and tied to trees.

"You're sure you're ready for this?" Detective Sergeant Michelle Ouellette asked without looking at him. She pulled her dark hair back into a short ponytail, clipped her gold badge to her belt, and snapped on a pair of bright blue latex gloves. All business. She was a sharp dresser, in a crisp men's dress shirt, with mother-of-pearl cufflinks. Turning up the collar of her raincoat against the wet, she resembled half the stylish women in town. Except for the cobalt gloves.

Lennox nodded. In last year's L. L. Bean barn coat and a tweed cap, with sandy hair in need of a trim, he looked like a high school English teacher. Standing under a large umbrella pulled from the back seat of the unmarked departmental Crown Vic, he wondered just how official they looked huddled there. At least the umbrella was black, he thought, and so could conceivably be passed off as police issue.

"Detectives arrive on scene at 8:47am, Sergeant Ouellette, primary," she said in her usual deadpan, signing the crime scene log. She handed the pen over to Lennox and turned to the responding officer, asking, "Who found the body?"

Patrolman Mike Foley had been first on the scene, a gap-toothed recruit on the force just over a year; his uniform still seemed too big on him. He nodded to a white-haired man sitting in the back of the nearest cruiser, looking like someone's kindly grandfather, with a wet beagle in his lap; they wore matching raincoats the same color as the crime scene tape.

"Guy lives over there, on Witch Hill Road," Foley said, pointing to a blue house fronting the park. "He and Daisy were out for their morning walk when they found him."

Great, Lennox thought. His first case on his first day back on the job, and Foley had to be the responding officer. They exchanged awkward nods and Lennox took a step back. Ouellette was the primary; he'd let her talk to Foley. He still didn't know what to say to him.

"Guy doesn't look like he got there by himself," Foley said quietly.

"Keep the scene controlled," Ouellette replied.

Lennox got his own gloves out of a pocket and together they approached the body. His mind was already buzzing.

Foley was right, the man had not gotten there by himself. What Lennox saw was not the swollen purple face of a man who had taken his own life with a noose, but the pallid face of a victim dead long before the rope had been tied around his neck. It was a middle-aged man, pushing fifty, with graying blond hair and a long, lantern-jawed face. He might have been good-looking, but for Lennox, whatever had once animated that face, lighting it up and making it unique, was gone now, and he no longer looked like who he had been. Like who he had been just yesterday, probably. The man wore a suede jacket, with jeans and sneakers. Casual name brands, now all stained dark with the soaking rain and contrasting sharply with his stark white face.

The rope was tied around the throat with three or four tight overhand knots—clumsy granny knots made by someone else. Lennox could tell by the way they bit so deeply into the flesh. Someone had hauled the man up into place and left him hanging there, a pale husk amid trees ablaze with autumn.

Lennox dropped the umbrella and took a few steps uphill, crouching down on the muddy ground. Eye-level with the corpse now, the man stared blankly back. Stepping to the side, he could see the rear of the head was a bloody mess. He counted five nasty head wounds, "compressed fractures" as he knew the medical examiner would call them.

His breath caught in his throat.

He motioned for Ouellette to join him.

"*Merde*," she swore, and crossed herself. She usually cursed in Quebecois.

"Multiple head wounds on a staged body," he said.

"Why hang him down here?" Ouellette asked, thinking aloud. "I thought the executions took place at the top?"

"They did. There's mention of a cart of getting stuck halfway up, and the accused had to walk the rest of the way. And some historians don't think this is really the execution site," Lennox said absently, unable to take his eyes from the corpse. "Some of them think the hangings actually took place over—"

"Not helping," Ouellette said.

"With the rain the way it's been the last few days, I wouldn't want to try to get to the top of this hill at night," he said. Witch Hill Road looped through the neighborhood on the southern side of the hill, ending in a narrow dirt service road running up to the water tank. On a dark and rainy night, the unlit road would be far too treacherous to even attempt. "And someone would notice during the day."

Ouellette took charge. She dismissed the ambulance—there was nothing for the paramedics to do here—and gestured to a pair of uniforms nearby.

"You two, start knocking on doors in the neighborhood over there and find out if anyone saw anything last night. Take them," she indicated two more uniforms who were just arriving on scene. "Go."

She took a few steps away and began taking pictures on her smartphone. They had to wait for the medical examiner to arrive before they could thoroughly check over the body, so Lennox went to talk to the man who made the discovery. The wet beagle stretched out to sniff at him. Lennox wasn't a dog person. He put his hands in his pockets.

"I'm Detective Lennox, mister...?"

"Hughes," the old man snapped. "It's about god damned time you got over here. I'm freezing my ass off and the dog's getting antsy."

So much for the kindly grandfather.

"What brought you out in this rain today, Mr. Hughes?"

"Walking the damn dog. How long have you been a detective?"

"Long enough. So you were walking the dog and called the police when you saw the body?"

"Yeah."

"You didn't get close, though, right? You didn't touch anything?"

"God no. What am I, an idiot?"

"No, sir," Lennox said patiently.

"There was something was going on in the park last night. I couldn't sleep, rain kept me up. So I'm awake. Beer in one hand, remote in the other. And out the window, I see a car drive by and right into the park. Turned off the headlights as he went. Looked like he was heading for that spot. About ten minutes later, comes back out, flips on his headlights, and takes off."

"He?"

Hughes shrugged. "I guess. I mean, I couldn't see a damn thing. The rain."

"What kind of car?"

"The kind with no headlights on a rainy night."

There were no lights in the park. A car would vanish as it drove across the grass, swallowed by the darkness.

"Light? Dark? Big? Small?"

"Dark. Sounded like a diesel. Mercedes or something foreign, maybe."

"And what time was this?"

"About one."

"Okay, thanks, Mr. Hughes. You've been very... helpful. I'm going to have an officer take your statement down and then we'll send you home, okay?"

"About goddamn time."

"And... thanks again."

A small wave of personnel arrived, the usual suspects required to be present at any unattended death. Crime scene investigation and evidence control were handled by the state police; it minimized chain-of-custody questions if nothing else. The central facility was located some miles outside of Boston, with several satellite labs scattered across the Commonwealth—the nearest one to Salem was fifteen minutes away in Danvers. The only one of the new arrivals that Lennox recognized was with a crime scene tech—Johnson, a civilian, a short woman with bright green eyes.

"Please don't muck up my scene before I've even had a chance to see it," she smiled.

She hesitated when she saw Lennox, giving him only a quick nod that didn't mask her surprise at finding him there. She spent a few minutes surveying the area before she got to work. Lennox admired the slow care she took as she began combing the scene in search of evidence. She seemed quietly excited to have something to do.

The medical examiner was right behind her; he carried a bulky aluminum case, the contents of which Lennox didn't even want to think about. He circled the body cautiously, craning his neck up at it and muttering into a small tape recorder. He eventually motioned to two uniforms to help him lower the body and lay it out on a blue tarp under a canopy they had hastily set up, protecting the corpse from the steady gray drizzle. He opened his case and Lennox looked away; watching an ME work, picking and probing, taking swabs and samples and slides, always made him squeamish.

Lennox turned to the crowd gathering on the far side of the crime scene tape. It was approaching ten as even more gawkers arrived. Ouellette let him go; she wasn't always good with people, and often let him handle the talking. He made a quick study of the two dozen or more onlookers—he was good with faces, and never knew when he'd need to remember a face later.

"Did anyone see anything?" he called.

Blank stares, shaking heads, downturned eyes. Half of them had cell phones out now, taking pictures and probably calling friends to tell them what was going on out at Gallows Hill. Word traveled fast, and Lennox wondered how many of the people in the little crowd even lived anywhere nearby.

The only faces he recognized belonged to reporters—one from the *Advertiser*, the other from the *Argus*.

"The prodigal detective returns," one said. "Welcome back."

"Halloween season in Salem," Lennox shrugged. "All hands on deck."

"How about a statement, detective?" the other asked.

"Nothing I can tell you yet. Body of a middle-aged white male was discovered this morning by a man walking his dog at this location."

"It's always someone walking the damn dog," the reporter scoffed. "But I wasn't asking about that, I was asking about—"

"Yeah, no comment."

"Fine. So who is he?"

"Name withheld pending notification of the family," Lennox lied.

"Cause of death…?" the guy from the *Advertiser* asked with an eager grin.

"Suspicious," Lennox replied. To say the least. "Anyone with information is requested to contact the Salem Police Department—"

"Oh c'mon—that's it? Seriously?"

"Seriously. If I had anything to tell you, I'd tell you." Another shrug.

"Like hell."

The guy from the *Argus* shook a Marlboro from the box, offering it to Lennox. Small kindnesses would often pry loose nuggets of information; journalists knew this at least as well as cops did.

"I quit while I was out," Lennox said, with a guilty smile.

"Congratulations," the reporter said bitterly.

He crossed the muddy ground back to where the corpse lay on the tarp, a lifeless poppet. His socks were wet, and squished as he walked. His lungs ached, but in a different way from when he had still been smoking. He wanted a cigarette.

The ME was giving Ouellette his preliminary report.

"Male, white, middle-aged, showing marked exposure to the elements—he's probably been out here all night."

"Since about one," Lennox said.

"I can give you a better estimate on time of death when I get him back to the shop," the ME went on, clearly not happy at the interruption. "But going by his state of rigor and body temp, I'd say he's been dead twelve to twenty-four. Immediate cause of death, blunt force trauma to the back of his head—there are five depressed fractures there, and one of them even peeled back a flap of skin. See there? The hanging was post-mortem, maybe by a few hours."

"Okay," Ouellette said.

"And he wasn't killed here," Johnson said. "There's nothing indicating this was the scene of the crime. Looks like he was just left here. You have a second scene out there somewhere."

"Did you find anything at all?"

"Some tire tracks," she said, "but nothing useful. The rain washed them out. But I can follow them from entering there, coming here, and doing a k-turn and back out," her finger traced the route as she described it. "All I can really tell you is that it was some kind of car. And he hit the gas when he was leaving—you can see he tore up some grass there. "

"Okay. Thank you."

"I'm finished with him for now," the ME said, "if you want a closer look."

The detectives moved in. Ouellette crouched and checked the man's pockets, shaking her head when she found they were empty.

"No wallet, no ID, no keys," she said quietly. "John Doe."

"Can't be easy, can it?" Lennox asked. "Don't even know if he's a tourist or a local." Two weeks before Halloween, the odds were fifty-fifty. "Wait—what's that there on his palm?"

"Thought you'd be interested in that," the ME said over his shoulder, packing up his case.

On the man's left palm was a crudely-drawn green pentagram—crooked lines forming a five-pointed star in a lopsided circle. There was another on his right palm, no better drawn than the first and even more off-center.

"Tattoo?"

"Looks more like… green Sharpie marker, doesn't it?" Lennox asked.

Ouellette swore in French again.

Lennox noticed a thin gold chain around the dead man's neck. He gently tugged a small cross from beneath the man's sodden shirt.

"So, pentagrams and a cross? On a body left at Gallows Hill?" he looked at Ouellette. "That's… I don't even know what that is."

"If you're done," the ME said impatiently. "I won't be able to get to him until tomorrow morning, probably about ten. You'll be there?"

"I will," Ouellette nodded.

Even on his best days, Lennox wasn't sure he could handle being present for an autopsy. And especially not now. He was happy to let her go to without him.

Their John Doe was zipped into a body bag and loaded into the van, off to the medical examiner's lab in Boston. The little crowd, cops and civilians alike, began to disperse, heading for places warm and dry. Lennox and Ouellette climbed back into the car. He stared blankly out the rain-spattered window.

Salem, according to most sources, took its name from *shalom*, Hebrew for *peace*. It was a quiet place, more-or-less living up to the name, except during Halloween when thousands descended on the city. But even then, most of the police department's time was taken up with robberies, assaults, and petty crimes. Murders were all but unheard of; nobody gets killed in Salem today, he mused. It just didn't happen here. And they sure as hell didn't have green pentagrams on their palms if they did.

Who are you? he wondered, watching the medical examiner's van leave the park. How did you end up here?

"You okay?" Ouellette asked.

"Yeah. I mean no, but… yeah."

"Okay, then."

"I want a doughnut," he said, starting up the car.

"And right back on the job."

At a Dunkin' Donuts down the street from the station, he got a plain doughnut and a large coffee, decaf with too much milk and too much sugar. He said he didn't want to use the drive-through, that he didn't mind standing in line. Ouellette waited in the car.

Inside, he glanced around uneasily and removed a small blister pack of tablets from a coat pocket. He popped a pale pink pill through the foil backing and washed it down with the decaf that was still too hot to really drink.

The tablet contained half a milligram of a benzodiazepine. Alprazolam, brand name Xanax—he wondered where they came up with these names. The anti-anxiety medication prescribed by Dr. Morrow, the department psychiatrist, who had evaluated him and declared him fit to resume active duty. But she had also set up a schedule of weekly appointments. The next was the day after tomorrow.

He'd put up the bravest front he could at the crime scene, but—

It was raining again outside, and Ouellette beeped the horn impatiently. He gulped down the rest of the decaf and pulled the tweed cap down over his eyes.

It was the wrong time to have quit smoking.

Chapter II

THERE WAS A CASE FILE WAITING on his desk when he and Ouellette arrived back in the detectives' bullpen at the station.

"Welcome back, detective," Lieutenant Winters said with an unhappy smile. Lennox startled as the lieutenant suddenly loomed over him. Winters was a big man who moved with the precise grace of a dancing bear. "I must have missed you when you came in." It sounded like an accusation, but the most casual comment from him usually did.

Lennox's return to work earlier that morning, before the call came in about a body at Gallows Hill, had been greeted by only a few curt nods and murmured hellos. Barely an acknowledgement that he had been gone at all. Most had simply ignored him, or whispered and nodded in his direction and turned away. There was nothing unusual in that; he had always been the odd man out among the dozen detectives comprising the Salem Police Department's Criminal Investigation Division.

"Call came in at start of shift," Ouellette said. "We headed right out."

"Fine," Winters said. He pointed to the case file. "Lennox, I want you working on that."

"Yes, sir," he replied, sliding into the chair he had not occupied for over three weeks. He probably had the neatest desk in the department, a certain regimented order being drilled into him during his twelve-year Coast Guard career. A bright blue deck prism, a souvenir of his old life before he became a cop, sat atop a pile of paperwork.

When he had first arrived that morning and hoped no one was looking, he had opened the right-hand drawer and hidden a couple blister packs of Xanax under some legal pads there. He'd put his old marlinspike, another Coast Guard leftover, on top, closing the drawer and shuffling through a stack of memos and updates, trying to look nonchalant and knowing how badly he was failing.

Now he glanced at the name on the case file Winters had left for him.

Annalisa Paiva.

Every detective in the Criminal Investigation Division knew the name. Her murder was the department's most stubborn cold case, still unsolved six years after her body had been found, neck broken, in the Point neighborhood, a scruffy part of town. Over the past few years, every detective had logged some hours attempting to close her case, and all had been unsuccessful. Unfortunately for Annalisa Paiva, her case had long since gone from being one that haunted the detectives of the CID to being one that now simply annoyed them.

She had been the pretty eighteen-year-old daughter of parents who had emigrated from the Azores a few years after she was born. She was their only child. The family lived on the third floor of a worn brick building on Ward Street, on the edge of the Point. According to the file, her father Estacio worked various odd jobs and her mother Gloria worked as a hotel maid.

Annalisa was bright and a good student who had been accepted to Salem State on scholarship to study nursing. She didn't complete her first semester.

On a snowy December day, when Halloween was long gone and Salem was once again just another coastal New England city for a while, Annalisa's body was found at the bottom of a flight of concrete steps leading to a service entrance behind her family's tenement building. Her neck was turned at an angle that made the back of Lennox's throat tighten as he went over the crime scene photos in the file.

Her key was still in the building's front door, indicating that she had probably been taken by surprise. She had apparently struggled with her attacker, as her coat had been pulled open, scattering leather buttons in the snow, before that final fatal shove to the bottom of the stairs. At least that was how Detective Sergeant Edward Curwen, the original investigating officer, had read the scene, and Lennox saw nothing to make him disagree at the moment.

Curwen had retired five years ago, shortly after Lennox arrived in the CID. They had never worked a case together, so he couldn't say he knew the man at all. But Curwen had the reputation for being a dogged and thorough investigator, and Lennox knew that *dogged and thorough* trumped *smart* any day of the week.

Curwen's suspicion had quickly fallen on Antonio Ramirez, Annalisa's Puerto Rican boyfriend, who also lived in the neighborhood. It was one of the grim old maxims of police work—the first suspect was almost always the victim's significant other. Lennox was always chagrined when it turned out to be right.

But Antonio had something approaching an alibi for the night in question; he had been out drinking with his brother Carlos until after midnight. But no one, least of all Edward Curwen, placed much faith in an alibi offered by a suspect's brother.

The residents of the Point did not take the news well, and the inevitable parade of community leaders—some long recognized, some newly self-styled—made speeches, demands, and accusations as tempers frayed. The streets of the neighborhood were tense for months, and Lennox was relieved to be promoted to the CID just as the investigation ground to a standstill; people were throwing things out of windows at uniformed officers in the Point, and the worst that detectives had to put up with was finger-pointing and frosty glares. Usually.

Being saddled with a cold case, a case that had for so long defied closing—Lennox knew he was being benched, given busywork to keep him out of the way. The department psychiatrist may have signed the papers and checked the boxes declaring him fit to return to duty, but clearly the Lieutenant hadn't made up his mind yet.

He bit his lip, realizing he was now working on *two* murders his first day back.

"There won't be much to do until the autopsy results are in tomorrow," Ouellette said quietly. "Get started on that, and I'll let you know when I hear."

"Thanks."

The next morning, Lennox rang the bell at an apartment house on Ward Street. The file gave this as the Paivas' address six years ago, and a quick check of the phone listings confirmed they still lived here. He rang the bell again and stepped back, looking up the face of the building. It was one of a number of tired old brick tenements along the street dating back to the First World War.

The Point had been an immigrant neighborhood for as long as anyone could remember, and probably longer. It was once the home of French-Canadian mill workers, but the last of the mills had closed over fifty years ago, the Quebeckers moved out, and the face of the neighborhood changed. New Spanish-speaking arrivals from Puerto Rico and the Dominican Republic moved in and *La Pointe* slowly became *El Punto.* Now it loomed in the imagination as a place where you couldn't walk down the street after dark, where you wouldn't hear a word of English spoken all day. But Lennox felt it was a neighborhood like most others, and most stories were exaggerated. The bark around here was generally worse than the bite. Generally. But he knew that the Point was far from perfect—it could be a rough place, and anyone looking for drugs could usually find what they wanted somewhere on the back streets of the Point. There, or on the Salem State University campus, probably.

But a Portuguese family in a Hispanic neighborhood made the Paivas outsiders amid outsiders, and some of Curwen's old notes in the case file showed he was aware of this. Apparently, he'd briefly considered the possibility of someone taking exception to what might have been seen as a forbidden Romeo-and-Juliet love, but quickly discarded the theory, settling on Antonio as his prime suspect.

An upstairs window banged open and a woman in a black housedress, dark hair in a tight bun, leaned out.

"*Quem está ai?*" she shouted.

Lennox held up his badge and called back, "*A polícia!*"

After several years on the force, he could identify himself as a police officer and even Mirandize a suspect in four languages.

The woman scowled and slammed the window shut. A moment later he heard her coming down the stairs and she opened the door.

"What do you want?" she asked.

Lennox guessed she was a few years older than he was, but she looked much older. Careworn. Up close, he saw her dark hair was heavily shot with gray, her face lined and tired. The face of a woman who had lost her only daughter.

"I'm here about Annalisa," he said awkwardly.

"She's dead," she told him, glaring at him like he was an idiot.

"I know, Mrs. Paiva. And I'm sorry for your loss. But I've been asked to look into her case. So if I could just come in and ask you a few questions? Or I can come back another time…?"

"No," she said, with an air of surrender. "Come up."

The apartment was tiny, smelling of furniture polish and boiling cabbage. It was all worn linoleum and chipped Formica, lime green and burnt orange, old and outdated but fastidiously clean. There were saints on the walls. Arranged along the top of the table under the far window were half a dozen photos of Annalisa, tracing her brief life from a sleeping newborn to a smiling young woman in a Salem State sweatshirt. A squat white candle stood at the end of the row of pictures. Lennox had no doubt that newspaper clippings covering the murder lay yellowing in the drawer below.

"So you think that man, Curwen, didn't do a good job?" she asked. Her accent was soft, probably much softer now, and her English much better, than six years ago.

"No, nothing like that. It's just that we don't like to see… cases… go unsolved. Nothing against Detective Curwen, but sometimes a fresh pair of eyes makes all the difference."

"So what do you want?"

"I'd like to go over a few things with you and your husband. Is he here?"

Gloria called into the bedroom and her husband slowly and painfully entered the cramped living room. He was a short and wiry man in a white t-shirt. He nodded to Lennox before lowering himself carefully on the couch, wincing as he did so. He smiled with embarrassment.

"He hurt himself at work," she said quietly. "He was moving boxes in a warehouse and did something to his back. He's been like this for two days, now. At home… at home, in the Azores, he is a doctor. Here, he moves boxes in a warehouse."

"Why don't you practice medicine here?" Lennox asked.

"No English; no good," he replied.

"His English is no good," Mrs. Paiva said. "Not good enough to pass the exams. He takes classes when we first get here, but can't learn it. So he does not practice medicine. So, the warehouse."

"Too old for English," Estacio said with another embarrassed smile.

"I'll try not to take up too much of your time," Lennox said. "Now, when the police came to tell you they had found Annalisa, what did you think had happened?"

"I thought someone had killed my baby," she said, again looking at him like he was an idiot.

"One of the first cases I ever investigated, I had to tell someone a relative had been killed, murdered," Lennox began slowly. "When I told her, she said 'oh my God, Joe did it.' And when we brought Joe in for questioning, he confessed. So… what I'm saying, Mrs. Paiva, is that if someone's name came to mind when you heard about Annalisa, I need to know."

"No," she said. "Nothing. No one."

"Okay. Detective Curwen mentioned a boyfriend, Antonio? Why would he have wanted to talk to Antonio?"

"There is no reason," she snapped. "Antonio is a good boy."

"Is, not was?"

"He comes to see me on Sundays. Every Sunday. He asks if I need anything. He... got married and they have a little boy now, two years old, but still he comes to see me every Sunday. And he tells me he misses Annalisa."

Lennox nodded. This could go either way. Antonio's visits could be seen as an indication of innocence, a sign that he felt connected to the family by the loss they shared. Or it could be fueled by a guilty conscience, trying to make up for what he had done. Or he could be visiting every Sunday to gloat.

"I think they had broken up," she added quietly.

"Really? Why is that?"

"She was quiet. He had not come to visit for a few weeks. I think she didn't know how hard school would be, and stopped seeing him a little after she started. She didn't say anything to me about it, but..."

"But a mother always knows."

She nodded. "She needed to concentrate on school. There would be time for boys later."

So Antonio was not just a boyfriend, but a spurned boyfriend. Curwen's instincts had been good.

"Where does Antonio live now?"

She gave him an address a few streets away.

"But he works around the corner," she added. "At the parking garage. He's the man in the booth."

Lennox glanced at his watch. "Would he be there now, do you think?"

"Probably."

"Okay, I think that's all for now. Is there anything else you can think of?"

"That man Curwen, he was not a nice man," she said.

"How so?"

"He did not like us, foreigners. He tried to hide it, but I could tell."

"Curwen," Estacio said sourly, shaking his head.

"He didn't care. Because we were not born here, and because Estacio's English is no good. So he didn't care about our daughter."

"I'm sorry he was like that. Can I ask you a personal question?'

She arched an eyebrow.

"Why do you stay? If your husband is a doctor at home, you could live a lot better than this. And you must have family back there. So why stay?"

"If we leave, it feels like we're… abandoning her. If the man who killed her is caught, maybe then. But now, it feels like we'd be leaving her, running away."

"Again, I'm sorry for your loss. I will be in touch. Thank you."

He nodded to Estacio on the couch and left his card. Downstairs, he let the door slam shut behind him as he walked around the back of the building to stand at the head of the concrete staircase where Annalisa's body had been found. Old leaves and trash had gathered at the bottom of the steps, piling up against the steel doorway.

Lennox was not a superstitious man, but the place gave him chills. It felt haunted, as though Annalisa Paiva, or some tiny part of her, did in fact still linger here in some weird way. He'd lived too long in Salem, he thought, where every street-corner was haunted by some Puritan, some witch, some ghost. Salem was too old and too storied for its own good.

His hand went reflexively to the jacket pocket where he used to keep his cigarettes and lighter. Now the pocket held a half-empty blister pack of Xanax. He shook his head. He needed a smoke, not a pill. Getting over the addiction was one thing, getting over the habit something else entirely.

He jumped when his cell phone rang. Ouellette.

"I'm back from Boston," she said. "With the reports."

Antonio would have to wait.

"All right. I'm underway. See you in a few minutes."

Chapter III

IT TOOK HIM TEN MINUTES to walk back to the station from Ward Street. Ouellette had stopped for a quick lunch on her way back. How she could grab a bite after attending an autopsy was beyond Lennox's understanding, but some things about Michelle Ouellette just were, even after being partnered with her for the last half-dozen years.

On other mornings, quieter mornings when there was no open case, they would follow a routine that had developed unspoken. After reading the day's newspapers and doing the Sudoku, she would hand them over to him; he preferred perusing the advice columns and doing most of the crossword before getting bored with it. But today wasn't a quiet morning.

"So what the hell was that out at Gallows Hill?" Detective Sergeant Fred Dworaczyk was asking as Lennox arrived back in the bullpen. Bald and beefy, with sixteen years on the force, Lennox had never once seen him without a Bluetooth jammed in one ear. Dworaczyk's eyes would hungrily follow Ouellette's every move from across the bullpen; just last week, she had dropped a file, and Lennox thought the man was going to pass out as she bent to pick it up. He seemed to regard Lennox as some sort of rival, scowling back angrily when Lennox asked about his wife and children in front of Ouellette. "I could not get over there—most of us were tied up in court on that drug case."

"John Doe," she replied. Canvassing the neighborhood around the park had yielded nothing; evidently, Hughes was the only one awake to have noticed anything on that rainy night. Running the victim's prints through the Integrated Automated Fingerprint Identification System returned no hits. "No identification yet."

She handed the medical examiner's report over to Lennox.

"Any surprises?" he asked, leafing through the write-up, trying not to pay attention to the more noisome details. He paused for a moment on the page detailing how the corneal opacity indicated a time of death between noon and eight o'clock on Sunday. His stomach fluttered and he turned the page.

"You have a cause of death?" Dworaczyk asked.

"Blunt force trauma to the head," Lennox asked, quoting the report, though Dworaczyk had directed the question to Ouellette. "Six depressed fractures, driving bone splinters into the brain. Massive intracranial bleeding..."

The report indicated that the weapon had been a heavy object, weighted at the striking end, like a hammer. But not a hammer, the ME noted; hammers did not leave the sharp right-angle wounds present on the body.

"What about the pentagrams on the palms?" Lennox asked.

"It's in there. Page five. Permanent marker, like you thought."

"The doer drew pentagrams on the victim?" Dworaczyk asked. "This place. Only in goddamn Salem."

"Not quite," Ouellette replied. "I checked, and there are several other cases where a murderer left pentagrams on or near the victim."

"So are you thinking serial killer?"

"Doubtful," she said. "The last case was eight years ago in Pennsylvania, and the pentagrams were drawn with the victim's blood. No cases on record mention permanent marker being used."

The medical examiner had found two sets of ligature marks on the dead man's throat. One was from the rope used to hang the body post-mortem; the victim had been several hours dead when someone tied that rope around his neck. But there was another ligature mark, indicating an attempt at strangulation. There were microscopic leather fragments found in the angry welt around the throat. Someone had attacked him with a leather cord.

"So someone tried to strangle him, and when that doesn't work—maybe he gets out—they bash him over the head," Lennox said, more to himself than anyone else. Ouellette nodded.

"Somebody wanted your guy very, very dead," Dworaczyk said. "How about stomach contents? Tox screen?"

"Baked goods, tea and/or coffee," Ouellette replied.

"Killed over Sunday tea," Lennox murmured. "All very Agatha Christie."

"Tox screen shows some heart medication. Nothing suspicious or unusual in a middle-aged male."

Johnson's report on the evidence collected at the scene had even less to say. While there were tire tracks to be found, the heavy rain had pummeled them all night long, blurring them into uselessness. The rope was a diamond-braided polypropelyne utility cord, half an inch in diameter.

"We'll find line like that in half the garages in town," Lennox said unhappily.

"Are you sure about that?" Ouellette asked.

"Yes. After twelve years in the Coast Guard, I know about line. That kind is common as dirt. Still, if we find a suspect, it'll give us something to try and match."

"So you already have this down as an *if*?"

Lennox ignored her and continued to skim the evidence report.

"Rug fibers found on the body," he said. The material and dyes marked it as an antique rug, according to the report "So he was wrapped up in a rug to move him. Classic."

And in conclusion, Johnson stood by her initial assessment that the murder itself had taken place elsewhere; she found nothing indicating that the park was their primary crime scene. It was certainly possible that the rain had sluiced away vital evidence—it had happened before—but she was usually able to find something when processing a scene. It was almost a point of pride with her. No matter how careful, criminals always made some telltale mistake, no matter how small. They dropped something, overlooked something, forgot something. But not out at Gallows Hill.

A female officer came down the hall and stood hesitantly at the opening in the half-wall that formed the CID bullpen.

"Detective Lennox?" she asked. "You wanted to see me?"

"Yes, Harker. Thanks for coming by. I need your opinion on something. Here, let me show you."

Officer Elizabeth Harker slowly crossed to Lennox's desk. The radio on her shoulder crackled and detectives a few desks away glanced over as she approached, puzzled. In any department, there was always a certain amount of friction between detectives and uniformed officers. Uniforms thought detectives were narcissists, and detectives often felt that uniforms were only fit to direct traffic. It was unusual for a uniform to set foot inside the bullpen.

And Harker wasn't just any uniformed officer. She was a minor celebrity around town, usually being interviewed by one TV station or another every Halloween. She was the only openly-practicing Wiccan in the department. If there were other Wiccans on the force, they served silently. Still in the broom closet, as Harker herself would have quipped. Her openness had long ago forced her into the position of being the unofficial liaison between the police and the local Wiccan community. And as such, she had never been completely accepted by either group.

In person, she was a tall, athletic woman in her thirties, with blonde hair and bright blue eyes. All very telegenic. With nine years on the force, the only outward sign of her religion was a pair of modest pentagram earrings she occasionally wore, the sort available in half the shops in town. That, and a triple-moon tattoo on her left shoulder blade. Lennox had seen it a few times in the station's gym, peeking out from under Harker's narrow tank top.

"This is my partner, Sergeant Ouellette. We're working on that body found over at Gallows Hill yesterday."

"Yeah, I heard about that," Harker said.

Lennox wondered for a moment if she had heard from fellow officers or fellow witches.

"When we examined the body, we found this."

He slid a photograph from the case file. A closeup of the man's left palm, with the green pentagram scrawled across it. She studied it for a moment before handing it back to him.

"Is that Sharpie marker?" she asked.

"According to the medical examiner."

"Why would someone do that?"

"I was kind of hoping you could tell us."

Harker scowled. "It's not part of established Wiccan practice," she said. "You might have some wacko solitary practitioner out there pulling shit like that, but it isn't mainstream Wicca."

"So we may be dealing with some lone weirdo?" Ouellette asked.

"Or someone's screwing with you."

"So would someone have done this to him, or would he have drawn them himself?"

"Like I said, I've never even heard of anyone doing this before. Sounds more like something out of a werewolf movie, you know?"

"Victim was also wearing a cross," Lennox said.

"Pentagrams *and* a cross?" she laughed. "Yeah, someone's screwing with you."

"Okay. Any reason someone would leave a body out at Gallows Hill?"

"Have you checked Cotton Mather's alibi?" Harker asked sourly.

"We're really not looking at him for this."

"Okay, the only thing that goes on out at Gallows Hill nowadays is baseball games. Tourists do come out, sure, but we aren't even sure that's the site of the executions."

"But... local witches do hold gatherings out there."

"Yes. But it's just become a kind of symbolic, you know? We need a place, and tradition says that's it, even if we know it might not be. Most Christians know Jesus wasn't born on December twenty-fifth, right? But that's what tradition says, so you go with it."

"One other thing."

He slid the photo of the dead man from the file. The victim lay on the ME's aluminum slab over in the morgue. The lighting was too harsh, and the face was disturbingly blue-white. Lennox never understood those who said the dead looked peaceful, or asleep. To him, dead people just looked dead.

"You recognize him?"

Harker rolled her eyes. "Yeah, we all know each other."

"Had to ask. Can you ask around about him? See if anyone in your… community… heard anything? We're just looking for some kind of angle here."

"There are a few people I can check in with. Give me a day or two and I'll see what I can find out for you."

"Great. I appreciate it. Thanks, officer."

"Sure. Blessed be."

Chapter IV

"So HOW IS YOUR FIRST WEEK BACK TREATING YOU?"
Dr. Morrow asked.

"It's good to be back on the job," Lennox said. "Good to have something to do again. The time off helped, but… it also gave me a little too much time alone in my head, you know?"

Linda Morrow was the Harvard-educated forensic psychiatrist the Salem Police Department kept on retainer, and she performed a variety of services for them. She helped in the psych evaluations of both new recruits and suspects, was called upon to do occasional criminal profiling, and offered counseling to officers as needed. She had probably seen half the department at some point or other, though few would have admitted it. Many officers who scheduled appointments with her were required to do so, and counseling was not something cops went to, or admitted to if and when they did.

Lennox had been ordered to undergo an evaluation in September; standard procedure after an officer-involved shooting. In a quiet city such as Salem, few officers even drew their weapon in the course of a twenty-year career, and no other officer in the history of the department had ever fatally shot a suspect.

In their first session, Lennox had curled up at the far end of the leather couch and insisted he was fine, and she knew immediately that he was unfit to return to duty. A few sessions later, when he finally admitted he was still "rattled" by what had happened, adding that he was having trouble sleeping, she wrote a prescription for Xanax and knew they were making some progress. Some.

He'd been on administrative leave for a week before the the attorney general decided it was not a criminal shooting and he would not be sending charges to the grand jury. Morrow knew he still wasn't ready to go back yet and set up a schedule of twice-weekly appointments; a blister pack of pills replaced the box of cigarettes in his coat pocket.

Her office was a few quiet streets away from the station, upstairs in an office building, at the end of a hall hung with calm Ansel Adams prints. The fluorescent lights in the drop ceiling were never on, and the office was illuminated instead by a few nondescriptly modern lamps in a way Lennox supposed was meant to be soothing. The walls were all pale pastels and she had a little gurgling electric fountain, with faux river stones, on her desk, and that was probably meant to be soothing as well, but he just found it oddly distracting.

"Being alone in your head too much has always been kind of a problem for you."

He nodded. "True."

Morrow glanced at her notes, scrawled across a yellow legal pad, double-checking a name.

"Ellen always said so."

Lennox closed his eyes and nodded at the mention of his ex-wife's name.

"Yes, she always said so."

His time on leave had given him entirely too much time by himself, and he had never quite mastered the art of being alone. Being forced to spend time sitting alone in a still half-unpacked apartment, with no one to talk to, starting to read a new crime novel every night, only to abandon it after the first chapter, sharply underscored how alone he felt, even almost a year after the divorce. Being off the job, with no case to work on and nothing to distract him, only let him again and again and again replay in his mind the shooting that had led to his leave.

For about a week, he decided to get out of the empty apart-ment, out of Salem altogether, and he drove over to Marblehead where, for a time, he became that sullen, unshaven ghost in the back corner of this or that coffee shop, staring blankly at passersby. Eventually, he realized that being in a busy place, listening to a dozen or more conversations, watching the intersections and deflections of a dozen lives, was depressing him more than staying locked and hidden in his apartment. He'd become jealous of these strangers, these carefree people carrying on with their lives despite whatever lay hidden behind their faces. He envied them. And that was when he realized it was probably time to go back to work, or at least to try. But he continued to schedule sessions with Morrow.

"Have you been in touch with Ellen?" she asked.

"No," he said. "Allison texted me yesterday, though."

"And how is she?"

"Stressed about midterms," Lennox said. Allison, his daughter, was a freshman across town at Salem State, the same university where, awkwardly, Ellen taught in the history department. Allison was the same age that Annalisa Paiva had been when she was killed, and the thought of it made the too-familiar knot in his stomach tighten again.

"And back to you," Morrow said. "I saw you quoted in the newspaper yesterday."

"Right. In the *Argus*. When I got back, the Lieutenant assigned me a cold case to work on, but a call came in—the body over at Gallows Hill—and my partner brought me in on that So, two cases my first day back. Two murders."

"And you got right back to work," she smiled. "I'm proud of you, Andrew. You should be proud, too."

"Yeah. I'm just beside myself."

"So, are you glad you went back? You were pretty hesitant just a few weeks ago."

That had been the question that had stalked him from one coffee shop to another, never far behind. Should he go back on the job? Or had the time come to quit? What else would he do? Would he even stay in Salem? Did he want to go back? Could he?

"I'm still not sure," he said quietly.

Ouellette was on the phone when he got back to the bull-pen. She nodded and spoke quietly, jotting notes. She passed a followup sheet over to him.

At this point in the season, the number of tourists and day-trippers in Salem grew by the day, and they would soon outnumber the residents if they didn't already. She had decided to work from the assumption that their John Doe was a tourist, and sent uniforms out to distribute flyers at the various hotels and tourist spots around town. Officers took down contact info for anyone who might have information about the man and passed the lead onto the CID for followup. This sheet gave the name of Ed Fuller, the security manager over at the Hawthorne, a posh downtown hotel. *The* posh downtown hotel.

Fuller was a retired Salem cop. He had put in his papers the minute he hit the twenty-year mark and settled right into the comfortable office downstairs at the hotel. He had still been in the CID when Lennox started as an officer, but had retired by the time he made detective, so they'd never worked together, but still knew one another in that Masonic way cops had. Lennox reached for the phone.

"Ed, it's Andrew Lennox over at the department. One of our officers indicated we should follow up with you."

"Yes. It's about that body you found."

Lennox's hand tightened on the receiver. "Yes?"

"We had a guest check in last Friday for a three-day stay. He didn't come to the desk to check out Sunday—that's not too unusual, some people just leave without coming by the desk. But when housekeeping opened the room that afternoon, all of his belongings were still there—clothes, suitcase, everything. But there's been no sign of him since Saturday."

"Really?" He reached over and knocked on Ouellette's desk to get her attention. She hung up her phone and waited.

"Yeah. He never showed up… and then I saw in the paper about the body you found. Even if it isn't Mr. Mather, I thought maybe you'd want to come take a look anyway."

"Mr. Mather? Like… like Cotton Mather?"

"Paul Mather. From Columbus, Ohio."

"Everything is still there?"

"Yeah, everything."

"Don't touch a thing. We'll be right there."

The Hawthorne was a ninety-three room luxury hotel, a local landmark that had held court in downtown Salem since the summer of 1925. Lennox had always admired the smooth Jazz Age elegance of the red brick façade. The restaurant, inevitably named Nathaniel's, had been a special-occasion stop for him and Ellen when they were still married. They went there to celebrate when she got tenure, and again when he made detective. He hadn't set foot in the building since the divorce, and now shook his head sadly as he and Ouellette passed a handful of tourists lingering outside the front door, savoring their cigarettes. Ever since he quit, he seemed to be living in an elegant film noir world where everyone smoked and looked fabulous as they did.

The lobby was decorated for the season with jack-o-lanterns and witches, black cats and skeletons. They were shown down to Fuller's office.

Fuller was a tall black man with salt-and-pepper hair and a close-trimmed beard. He had no doubt put on weight since his days with the department, but still looked trim in a double-breasted suit. He shook Lennox and Ouellette's hands with a firm grasp and a genuine smile, happy to see a couple of cops despite the circumstances.

"So what can you tell us?" Lennox asked.

"Not much more than I said on the phone," Fuller said. "We had a guest, Mr. Mather, check in on Thursday afternoon, and he was scheduled to stay through to Sunday. As of one o'clock on

Sunday, he had not come by the front desk to check out and leave his keycard. Like I said on the phone, when housekeeping opened the room that afternoon, everything was still there."

"So what did you do?" Ouellette asked.

"We put a lock on the room, so if he came back he wouldn't be able to get in and would have to come by the desk if he wanted his stuff. Standard procedure. By Monday noontime, he hadn't shown, and we assumed he'd taken off sometime Sunday. His car was missing."

"This didn't seem suspicious?"

"No, actually. People do sometimes take off in the middle of the night. You wouldn't believe the things that go on in a hotel," Fuller said, shaking his head slowly.

Lennox chuckled. "Maybe, maybe not."

"Last year, a guest got a phone call in the middle of the night—bad news from back home. He got dressed, got in the car, and drove right back to Montpelier that night. He called a couple of days later and asked us to FedEx the belongings he'd left in his room. Jackass. So, it happens, and didn't seem suspicious at first."

"Do you have Mather's information?"

Fuller handed over a printout.

"Mr. Paul J. Mather of Columbus, Ohio," Lennox read. "Reserved a single non-smoking room, king bed, two weeks ago. Two weeks ago? Seriously?"

Hotel rooms in Salem for the month of October sold out a year or more in advance. Getting a room two weeks before Halloween at any downtown hotel, let alone the Hawthorne, was a minor miracle.

"We had a cancellation."

"Says here he checked in Thursday. He was here alone?"

"Yes."

"No… company while he was here?" Ouellette asked.

"We have a couple of regular girls and one regular guy. I checked with them and nobody saw him," he said. "And they know better than to lie to me or I'll ban them from the property. They make good money at this hotel, and I'll leave them alone as long as they keep a low profile and play ball."

"Does anyone on the... regular staff... remember seeing him?"

"Karen checked him in."

"We'll need to see her," Ouellette said. "Now, please."

Fuller buzzed the front desk and asked for Karen to be sent down.

"Car's listed as a blue Prius with Mass plates, so probably a rental," Lennox looked up from the printout. "It's gone?"

"That's why we thought he must have just taken off. You don't assume a guest is lying dead somewhere."

Karen was a nervous goth college girl. Lennox wondered how many piercings she had to take out before they let her work the front desk.

"Hi, Karen, I'm Detective Lennox." He slid the morgue photo of their John Doe from his leather organizer. "Is this the man you checked in? Is this Mr. Mather?"

"Oh my God," Karen breathed. "Yeah. That's totally him."

"Let's see the room," Ouellette said.

Upstairs, Lennox and Ouellette waited in the door with Fuller, scanning the room while waiting for Johnson to finish processing it.

Rooms at the Hawthrone were slightly smaller than Lennox might have imagined. Nice but unremarkable. The walls were dark blue and the bed had a muted floral print spread. The furnishings were the usual desk, chest-of-drawers, and armchair that almost matched and were somewhere between elegant and quaint. Overall, it was probably indistinguishable from a million other hotel rooms with interchangeable comforts. The heavily-curtained window looked out over the green expanse of the Common several stories below.

"This isn't your murder scene, either," Johnson said without looking up from whatever she was doing. "I can tell you that right now. This carpet does not match the fibers I recovered from the body, and there's no blood anywhere. There are some… fluids on the sheets, but I bet you a dollar they aren't from him. Some stuff never really comes out in the wash. This is why I never stay in hotels. Hotels are gross."

"Nice," Lennox said. "Thanks for that."

"C'mon in. I'm done here."

It only took a few minutes of going through over the room to discover there was nothing to find. There was nothing left in the pockets of the jeans and khakis draped over the chair, tucked into the pages of the visitors' guide, or hidden between the mattresses. Lennox asked if Mather had used the room phone, or placed anything in the hotel safe. He had done neither.

They found nothing remarkable, nothing indicating who he was or what he was doing in town.

"So why was he here?" Lennox asked.

"Tourist," Ouellette said. "We get them here this time of year."

"But he's not a tourist," Lennox said with another glance around the room.

Ouellette nodded. "Right. No brochures, no souvenirs."

This time of year, no one could walk down the street without having a dozen flyers and coupons thrust at them, advertising psychic readings, haunted houses, and ghost tours.

Leaving the hotel, the detectives passed the bronze statue of Nathaniel Hawthorne, Salem's favorite son. Tourists in pointy plastic witch hats posed and mugged for pictures at the statue's smooth granite pedestal. Hawthorne sat, hand on hip, as though he were momentarily pausing to admire the sunset on a long walk. Lennox was certain that he must still be meditating on the nature of sin and guilt all these years later.

Back in the bullpen, Lennox entered Paul Mather's name into the National Crime Information Center. The NCIC, another database maintained by the FBI, listed information about every kind of crime and criminal activity imaginable. It was where Ouellette had searched for "pentagrams" earlier. The sheer amount of data available, the interconnectedness and level of cooperation and intelligence-sharing between departments across the country that it allowed, always struck Lennox as faintly miraculous. But as the brain child of J. Edgar Hoover, it also gave him a weird intellectual chill, and seemed a little too Big Brother at times.

Running Paul Mather's name immediately returned a missing person report from the Columbus PD, filed earlier that morning. Mather, age 48, was employed as an auditor with the sprawling investment empire that was the Lyons Financial Group, a bank that owned other banks. He had been reported missing yesterday, on Tuesday, when he failed to report to work for the second day in a row. Detective Jack Simpson of the Columbus PD was given as the primary contact in the case.

The report included a copy of Mather's Ohio driver's license photo. It was their John Doe. Despite the usual forced calm of a driver's license, Mather's eyes were bright, his face ruddy with life. He seemed to be holding in a smile, as though the bored DMV photographer had made some joke just before snapping the picture. Here, at least for Lennox, was proof that Paul Mather, whoever he was, had been a living and breathing person—some-one who once waited in line, laughed at jokes. Proof that he had once been more than just a corpse on a slab.

Lennox printed out the photo and put it next to the pallid morgue photo.

At her desk across from him, Ouellette had Googled Mather, and bit her lip.

Paul Mather left almost no digital footprint. Ouellette found nothing online, aside from the occasional professional member-ship listing or announcement that he had won this or that award from various accounting and auditing organizations. No blog, no social media, no snarky comments left on so much as a single discussion forum that she could find. She was quietly frustrated; like Johnson, Ouellette could usually uncover something when she went looking for it.

"Doesn't Lyons own a bunch of banks?"

Ouellette tapped and clicked and nodded. "Over thirty... including First Colony."

"Which is over on Washington Street," Lennox smiled. "We may have something."

Lennox picked up his phone and punched in the number of the Columbus PD.

"Sergeant Simpson? This is Detective Andrew Lennox of the Salem PD, out in Massachusetts. We found Paul Mather's body in town on Monday morning. It's a homicide, sorry to say."

"Oh, damn."

"Um, yeah, sorry," he said awkwardly.

"What happened?"

"We're still working on that. What do you have on him?"

"Not much more than I put into the system. He took Thursday and Friday off work, didn't say where he was going, and then didn't show up on Monday. Didn't answer his phone, and then somebody from the office went by his house, nobody home. They called his sister, she didn't know anything, so she reported him missing."

Lennox scrawled down the sister's phone number as Simpson read it off.

"I know this is a weird question, but do you have anything on his religious background?"

"Um, no. Some kind of Protestant? Hasn't come up. Why?"

"Well, you know Salem attracts all kinds of occult types. We found him out at Gallows Hill, which is where they supposedly used to hang the witches. It's probably not, but... well, anyway, I don't know if he had any connection to witchcraft or occult practices?"

"No clue," Simpson laughed.

"When we found him, he had pentagrams drawn on his hands."

"Pentagrams?" Simpson asked incredulously.

"Yeah, a star in a circle. It's a witch thing. We probably see it here more than you do."

"Yeah, probably."

"So I was wondering about his background."

"He was an accountant," Simpson said, the best he could come up with.

"Right."

"Have you pulled his cell phone records?"

"I put in the request, but the carrier says it could take a week. Idiots. They should be able to push a couple of buttons and have it."

"Can you let me know when you have those? I need to know who he might have been talking to here."

"Sure."

"Okay, thanks."

He hung up and rubbed his hands over his face.

"So," he said to Ouellette. "We have a dead man named Mather, with his head knocked in, hanging at Gallows Hill, with pentagrams on his hands and a cross around his neck. And he's a Luddite accountant from Ohio."

"Ready to go back out on leave?" she asked.

"Just about," he sighed, dialing the sister's number. Voicemail.

"Hi, this is Danielle, leave a message…" Beep.

"Danielle, this is Detective Lennox with the Salem Police Department in Massachusetts. I'm calling about your brother, Paul. Please call me as soon as you get this message. I'll give you my office and cell numbers…"

He hung up and stared at the phone for a long moment.

"So that went well," he murmured.

They agreed to meet at First Colony when they opened tomorrow at nine. As Lennox left the station and walked home down the brick sidewalks, a slinky black cat ran out of a doorway. They paused at the sight of one another.

"Go ahead," he said to the cat. "You know you want to."

The cat crossed his path and vanished over a wall across the street.

"Yeah, great."

Chapter V

First Colony Bank occupied a starkly brick building with long narrow windows protected by wrought iron bars that twisted and curled elegantly. It was a new building trying to fit in with older surroundings, but still holding itself somehow aloof, distancing itself from the witch kitsch that ruled so much of downtown, the herb shops and tarot readers that brought the tourists who brought their wallets.

Inside, the only people in line were two women in velvet capes and sweeping skirts, with that witchy gothic hippie look so popular in town. They were sorting out something with the business teller. Ouellette showed her gold badge to another teller and asked to see a manager.

A man named Alan Barbour appeared a moment later, and discreetly steered the detectives through some security doors, past a few guards, and finally into his upstairs office.

"So what can I do for you?" Barbour asked nervously.

Lennox brought out the photo of Paul Mather. Barbour took off his glasses and scrutinized it, then handed it back with a puzzled expression.

"We're investigating a homicide," Ouellette said. "This man worked for your parent company, Lyons Financial. We were wondering if he had been here in the last few days."

"Why would he come in here?" Barbour asked, replacing his glasses. They had designer titanium frames, tiny and square, and Lennox thought they looked a little too sleek for a bank manager. Barbour glanced over Ouellette, but was probably just calculating how much more expensive her dress shirt was than his. Lennox thought he saw a flash of envy when Barbour noticed her tiger's eye cufflinks.

"We were hoping you could tell us that."

Barbour's eyes went back to the photo.

"Wait a minute—that's Paul Mather, isn't it?"

"Yes."

The bank manager blinked.

"Oh my God—this is who you found a few days ago."

"We're trying to find out what he was doing here in town," Lennox said.

"He wasn't here on bank business, I can tell you that."

"You're sure?" Ouellette asked.

"Absolutely. If he was coming to First Colony on official business, I would have been notified, and I didn't get any notification. I never even met the man."

"But you recognized his photo."

"Yes… well, a lot of us would," he said uncomfortably. "You might want to talk to Kevin Kelly."

"Who's that?"

Barbour sighed and said, "He's one of our guys who transferred in from the Columbus office."

"He knew Mather?"

"You really should talk to him yourselves…"

Kevin Kelly had a round face and dark blond hair that stuck out artlessly in every direction. While he was somewhere in his thirties, he still had the air of a frat boy whose partying days weren't too far behind, despite the wedding band and suit. Lennox immediately knew Kelly for a smoker—he could smell it on him; the last traces of the morning smoke break still clinging to his jacket, making Lennox's mouth water. They walked him across the hall to an empty conference room and shut the door.

"We're investigating the death of a Mr. Paul Mather here in town," Ouellette said. "We understand you knew him back in Ohio."

"Yeah, but… wait—he was here?"

"Yes."

"What was he doing here?"

"We were hoping you could tell us that."

"I don't think he came looking for me… I mean, unless he did. Asshole."

"So you two weren't on good terms, obviously?"

Kelly dropped into a chair.

"I really shouldn't go into any of this," he said. "I don't have to."

"Kevin, you can either tell us what the story is, or we can spend a couple of days finding out what it is on our own," Lennox said. "If we have to go and do that, it's not going to make us happy. It's not going to make us like you."

"Okay. Okay. You must already know what happened or you wouldn't be here though, right?"

"Kevin," Ouellette warned.

"Back in the Columbus office, there was a… clique. We'd hang out after work, hit the bars, the strip club, whatever. We were all kind of the young Turks, you know? Making way too much money and we kind of got stupid."

Lennox bit his lip. Kelly and the boys were probably getting bonuses as everyone else lost their last cent.

"And stupid means greedy in this case, doesn't it?"

"Yeah."

"And?"

"Really shouldn't be talking about any of this…"

"Kevin," Lennox knocked on the conference table to get his attention. "We are not from the SEC. We are investigating a *homicide*."

"Okay, fine. There were some… misappropriations."

"Of…?"

"Customer funds. We each started skimming a little bit from a few of our accounts, just a little salami slice, coupla bucks here and there, no one would even notice it. But it added up, and... we used it to do some trading on our own."

"And Mather caught you."

"Yeah. Mather caught it."

"How much did you... misappropriate?" Lennox asked.

"One point one million," Kelly replied.

"You are kidding me."

"Nope." Kelly tried not to smile as he said it.

"So what happened?"

"Well, he caught me and a couple others in the clique, and we all got sent down to internal auditing, and they wanted us to name names. Everybody was pointing fingers at everybody else, even people who had nothing to do with anything. It was all pretty messed up."

"It turned into a witch hunt," Lennox said.

"Yeah, I guess."

"So you were caught misappropriating funds and you still have a job because... why exactly?"

"Nobody was going to get fired over an amount like that," Kelly said. "We didn't steal anything—"

"You just misappropriated it," Ouellette observed.

"Lyons didn't want the publicity. You don't want customers knowing about messed-up behind-the-scenes shit, so they swept it under the rug and we all got reassigned."

"Like pedophile priests?" Ouellette asked.

Kevin Kelly just scowled.

"And Mather was responsible for all that. Because of him, you ended up in some podunk Massachusetts town and now everyone back home thinks you commute to work on a broom. And that's his fault."

"So when you heard he was in town..." Lennox said.

"I had no idea he was even here!"

"But if you did—?"

"If I did, I sure as hell wouldn't have killed him."

"Because?" Ouellette demanded.

Kelly was breathing hard, like a running man.

"Look, my parents live in Boston. About the time all that shit started to go down, my dad got sick—another reason to think about a transfer. There were no openings in Boston but there was one here. So at least I get to be near my folks if they need me. And then Mom hired a visiting nurse for a few days a week, and she ends up being totally hot, so..."

Kelly took out his wallet and showed them a photograph in a clear plastic sleeve. Him, in a tuxedo, next to a striking redhead in a short white wedding dress. They both held champagne flutes.

"We're expecting a son in February," he beamed.

"And you're going to name him Paul?" Lennox asked, as a solid lead evaporated.

"No. Look, all I'm trying to say is, he wasn't my friend, but I got no reason to kill him. The guys who went to jail got what they deserved, and things got crazy for me for a little while but I landed on my feet. And we're naming him Richard, after my Dad."

"Congratulations," Ouellette said.

"So, what was he like?" Lennox asked.

"I didn't know him real well. He wasn't part of the clique, you know? That was a real thing with him, he was definitely not part of the gang."

"Unfriendly?"

"Yeah. Aloof. He was an auditor, you know? He wanted everything to add up and balance. He was kind of intense. I heard his wife died, and I guess he took it pretty hard."

"Okay, thanks for your time," Lennox said.

Elizabeth Harker was waiting for them when they got back to the bullpen.

"I checked with the usual suspects, as it were, and nobody knows nothing," she said. "Nothing about the guy and no one can think of a reason why a body would be left out at Gallows Hill. And nobody understands the pentacles on the hands. Consensus of opinion is that it's some wacko trying to make it look like there's a Wiccan connection."

"Yeah, I was coming to that conclusion myself," Lennox nodded. "Our guy is an auditor from Columbus; doesn't seem real Wiccan to me."

"Oh, you'd be surprised," Harker said. "I found a new plumber at a Full Moon Circle. We're not all named Owlmoon Ravenshadow, you know. We don't all run herb shops."

"Our guy was wearing a cross, which doesn't seem like a real Wiccan thing to do, and like you say, Wiccans don't draw pentacles on their palms. My guess is that one of these things is legitimate and the other is planted. I bet you a cup of coffee the cross is really his, and the pentacles are planted."

"Or they were both planted and someone's really trying to screw with you," Harker nodded. "Do you have a name yet?"

"Funny you should ask. Paul Mather."

"Mather? Like Cotton Mather? Really?"

"Yeah."

"A name like that would make him unpopular with some people around here."

Mather was the Puritan theologian who many saw as the face of the witch trials. Lennox knew that once again, history and legend did not quite agree, and Mather may not have been the fire-and-brimstone fanatic painted by tradition. Twenty-nine years old when the trials began, Mather had been very much a man of his time, deeply devout and immersed in the harsh Puritan worldview, but a formidable intellectual and prolific author nonetheless. While he remained unrepentant of the role he had played during the witch trials, some historians argued that he had actually been a mitigating influence as hysteria swept region, and things may have been even worse without his presence. But legend overran history like weeds, especially in a place like Salem.

Inwardly, Lennox had to admit to a certain small envy; Mather and the other extremists of old Salem Village lived in a world that worked according to rules, a world that made sense, where every single thing was a divine guidepost. Even if the rules were invisible, the results were not. Puritans had answers. Detectives were left in a senseless world without signs, without an overall plan. They only ever had questions.

"People might really get upset about that?" Lennox asked skeptically. "Kind of a long time ago now."

"True, but some people, that's like being named Hitler, you know? And some of them are a little self-righteous, and need a place to put their anger. Somebody else at my Full Moon Circle once went down to the cemetery in the North End where Mather is buried and pissed on his grave."

"Well, I hope he didn't get caught," Lennox shook his head.

"She didn't," Harker said with a poker face that rivaled Ouellette's.

"Based on what you had said before, I had been ready to discount any Wiccan connection, but if his name is Mather, doesn't that change things?"

"It could. Like I said before, you might be dealing with some wacko solitary practitioner, maybe someone who's still got… serious issues… with Cotton Mather. If your guy is a descendant, that might set somebody off. If they were crazy, mind you. Hanging Cotton Mather's great-great-great-grandson out at Gallows Hill is kind of the ultimate *fuck you*, you know?"

"Okay, so we're looking for a crazy person."

"Could be."

"Great."

"If I hear of anything, I'll let you know."

"Thanks."

He started tapping the marlinkspike against his desk as Harker left, sullenly thinking.

"Detective Lennox."

He startled. Lieutenant Winters, sneaking up on him again.

"Yes, sir?"

"How is Paiva coming?"

"Making steady progress and following up some promising leads, sir," he lied. And Winters knew it.

"Fine. Keep me informed of your... progress. And detective?"

"Yes, sir?"

"Tonight is crime watch meeting, and your name is next on the list."

"Really, sir? Crime watch? Pray, and what have I done to offend thee?"

The Lieutenant smiled and said, "Let me get my fucking notes."

Chapter VI

CRIME WATCH MEETINGS WERE HELD one Thursday a month in the auditorium downstairs at the station, and each month a different uniformed officer and detective were assigned to act as "community liaisons." The higher-ups felt that it helped with police transparency and accountability, and improved community relations. Each month, the assigned officers supplied increasingly creative excuses for being unable to attend, few of which ever worked. The meetings were usually poorly attended, with the same dozen or so loudmouths complaining about missing recycling bins, the damn tourists, the noisy neighbors, and old grievances they would never let be forgotten nor resolved.

Lennox got a pad and pens from his desk, and trudged downstairs for seven o'clock, ready to be introduced as that month's Community Liaison Officer.

When he opened the door to the auditorium, he realized tonight's meeting would be completely different.

The room was packed, standing room only. His heart sank as he scanned the crowd. Three city council members, and several local reporters were scattered around the auditorium, amid the usual gadflies, rabble-rousers, and concerned taxpayers. A couple of Boston news stations had set up cameras along the back wall; at a second glance, he noticed one from New York.

Worst of all, the mayor and the president of the city council were seated at opposite ends of the front row.

Tobias Pyncheon had been mayor of Salem for as long as anyone could remember. He was a scion of one of the city's old

45

money families, and with his bushy silver hair swept back from his square face, he had the good looks of a mildly scandalous movie star. He was known to be fond of single malt scotch, double-breasted silk suits, and expensive foreign cars, one of which—a soot-black Jaguar—was rakishly parked outside the station. Pyncheon lived in a home on the water with a bleach-blonde wife less than half his age.

At the opposite end of the row was Council President Jake-never-Jacob Gilman. Gilman's cargo pants and blue shirt, sleeves rolled up and tie pulled loose, were every bit as carefully chosen as Pyncheon's Italian suit, meant to underscore the man-of-the-people image that had won him his seat on the council. The shortcomings and excesses of the Pyncheon administration were his favorite target.

"Crap," Lennox murmured.

The meeting was called to order and the usual business was dispensed with quickly. Lennox was introduced and he rose stiffly to his feet, smiling, and feeling as thought he had just been thrown to a pack of very hungry, self-righteous wolves.

"What can you tell us about the body you found?" someone immediately called out.

"I am unable to comment on ongoing investigations, but we are working around the clock and pursuing several very promising lines of inquiry," he said, falling back on the traditional boilerplate. He wondered if he could possibly pop a Xanax into his mouth unnoticed. "We ask for your support and cooperation as we move forward with the investigation. If anyone has any information—"

"Who was he?" a voice called.

"Again, I cannot comment on an ongoing investigation, but—"

"You all know that my administration has always been tough on crime, and I have been in close touch with the Chief of Police and his men since Monday morning," Pyncheon said, sweeping to his feet and turning to face the cameras more than the crowd. "If I've said it once, I've said it a hundred times—Salem has the finest police force in the Commonwealth, and I know they are very close to making an arrest in this case. The streets of this city are safe, ladies and gentlemen, thanks to the hard work of our police officers—"

"Work you have made more and more difficult for them to do every year," Gilman shouted back. "The last budget the city council submitted to you increased funding to the police department and you *vetoed* it! It took months of negotiating before we could pass a budget because of you, and everyone in this city knows it. This great city is teetering on the brink because of the failed policies of the Pyncheon administration…"

Lennox closed his eyes. He remembered the budget in question, and the funding increase for the department had been minimal. It would never have covered the cost of hiring new officers; the department might have been able to afford a photocopier. Or a whiteboard. They were both, as usual, trying to be the hero and hoping that everyone forgot the details. It wasn't surprising that these two were using a man's murder to take shots at one another, but it was appalling. Pyncheon wasn't there to reassure the citizens—he was there because there were cameras. And Gilman was there because Pyncheon was there.

"We wish this unknown visitor to our city to be surrounded by white light as he takes his first steps on his last great journey," intoned Magnus Moon, slowly rising.

Magnus was a portly middle-aged man with long dyed-black hair and a melodramatic leather coat. And black Reeboks. Around his neck was a jumble of amulets, crystals, and pentagrams, and one hand rested on an ebony walking stick with a silver wolf's head handle. Magnus was a well-known local character, perennial candidate for various political offices, and utter egomaniac. Magnus always sounded strangely rehearsed, and Lennox could easily imagine the man practicing his delivery in front of a mirror at home.

"We can only hope the myrmidons of the police force are able to bring the evil-doer behind the deed to swift justice!" Magnus concluded, with a slight bow toward Lennox.

"We'll certainly do our best. We don't let people get away with murder in Salem. So again, if any of you have any information—"

"While you are here, inspector, might we once again raise the question of the offensive nature of the crass caricature which serves as the very symbol of your constabulary?" Magnus interrupted, pointing at the Salem PD emblem hanging from the podium at the front of the room.

The emblem was a silhouetted witch on a broom, with a flowing dress and conical hat. It appeared on every police officer's uniform, on the side of every cruiser, and on every sheet of departmental stationery, and had for years. Similar images could be found on sweatshirts, shot glasses, and signs hanging outside of half the businesses in town, and even on the water tank atop Gallows Hill. It was the target of Magnus's long-standing ire.

"Can we truly feel protected and served by a *gendarmerie* which openly mocks and trivializes the religious heritage and beliefs of a significant portion of our citizenry, inspector?"

Groans from the audience indicated that they had heard all this before.

"It's detective, actually," Lennox corrected, "and the emblem is a recognizable symbol of the police department, which neither mocks nor trivializes anything—"

"Oh don't even listen to him, detective," cried a voice in the crowd. "Everyone knows what a dingbat he is!"

"So you do have a suspect?" someone else asked.

"Again, I cannot comment—"

"Why won't you tell us... detective?" Magnus smiled suspiciously, and all but licked his lips.

"Oh shut the hell up," a woman in a flannel shirt yelled. "Things like this wouldn't happen here if you people weren't always trying to turn the city into a goddamn carnival."

"Do you know what it does to my property values to have a bunch of freaks across the street chanting at midnight?" a man called. Lennox recognized him; he'd seen him at these meetings before. His obsession with property values made him a weird kind of idiot savant.

"Property values in Salem have consistently risen every quarter for the last several years," Pyncheon interjected. "And Salem remains a world-class tourist destination, welcoming visitors from every corner of the globe."

"Freaks?" Magnus retorted. "Religious intolerance is alive and well in Salem, we see! Still trying to weed out the undesirables, are we?"

Lennox had never actually heard an audience boo someone before. Yeah, he thought, this is going really well.

"Oh, please. Nobody's trying to hang you, you *freak*."

The babble of angry voices echoed in the room as the torches and pitchforks came out. Lennox screwed his eyes shut, rapidly approaching the point where he wouldn't care if anyone saw him slipping a Xanax.

"Okay, thank you all very much," he yelled, trying to get some tiny measure of control back. "Does anyone else have anything?"

"So are you looking at the witches or not?" someone called. "I heard he had pentagrams on his palms. Think one of them could have did it? That's where I'd start if I was you guys."

"I heard he was some relative of Cotton Mather?" yet another voice called. "What about that?"

Lennox's breath caught in his throat. How did *that* get out? Dammit, Salem was too small. Everyone knew someone somewhere. Everyone had a cousin or an old high school buddy on the police force. Word would always get around.

"None of us have a hand in this business," Magnus Moon insisted, laying a pious hand upon his breast.

"I heard my neighbor arguing with someone on Sunday," a man said. "I got up to look out my window to see what's going on. I didn't recognize him, but I could probably identify him if I saw him again."

"You son of a bitch," the neighbor cried from the other side of the room. "You were all pissed off I put out my recycling too early last week and now you tell the cops I murdered someone?"

"Hey, I'm just saying you argued with someone and I haven't seen him since. Guilty conscience much?"

"That was my brother, jackass."

"So?"

"What about the woman in white?" an elderly woman in the third row asked. "Have you spoken to her?"

"No," Lenox replied. "Who are you talking about, please?"

"The last few nights, since you found the body, she comes out to the park and lights a candle on that spot. You haven't spoken to her yet? She must know something."

"We will talk to her. Anything else? Okay, thanks everyone."

He waded through the crowd, pushing through a side door into a dim corridor, only to find Mayor Pyncheon waiting for him. Pyncheon was a head taller, and loomed.

"Listen to me," the mayor said, lowering his face a few inches from Lennox's own. "This is a fucking tourist town, and if people think they'll get killed if they come here, they won't come here. Do you fucking understand? Figure this thing out. Arrest someone. Anyone."

Gilman closed the door quietly behind him as he entered. He folded his arms and looked on disapprovingly.

"I was just explaining to Detective Lennox here that we need to see an arrest. This week. And I hope he doesn't have to shoot anyone this time."

Pyncheon slammed the door behind him as he went.

Gilman shook his head.

"You know, for once I agree with that asshole," he said bitterly.

The clock on the bullpen wall showed 8:20 when Lennox arrived back upstairs. Being a detective in Salem was pretty close to a 9-to-5 job; there was usually no night shift and so the CID was dark and silent. He tossed his blank pad onto his desk and sighed, running his hands over his pale face. He had meant to take notes, but couldn't with all the interruptions and accusations and the politicians and Magnus Moon doing their usual big-man-on-campus act.

Well, that was a complete disaster, he thought. No useful information had come forward, just rumors and accusations, and he had been unable to calm the residents' fears. Half of them probably thought he was an idiot, and the other half probably thought he was keeping the real story from them. This was how hysteria started, he mused, how it spread to engulf an entire city, and Salem had seen enough of that already. Things changed so little in three centuries.

Goodwife Bacagalupi signed her name in the Black Man's book and doesn't sort her recycling...

And his appearance in front of a packed room of citizens and reporters, with news cameras rolling, speaking on behalf of the Salem Police Department, meant that his was now the face of the investigation in the public's mind. So... that was a disaster.

He reached into his drawer for a blister pack of pills, but put them down and slammed the drawer shut. He didn't want to admit just how badly he wanted one.

He left the station, and headed out to Gallows Hill Park. It was about a mile, and although much of it wasn't a particularly scenic route, he needed a walk.

When he first arrived in Salem almost a decade ago with his wife and their daughter, he had set out to walk down every street in the city, exploring his new home, committing it all to memory. It had taken six weeks, but he had done it, and now had a map of the city in his head. Then he took every walking tour in town. And when he had finished taking those, he read guidebooks, then history books—anything to help get a handle on his new city, his new home. And still, years later, being out in the old streets and lanes and squares, feeling the city beneath his feet, was always somehow soothing.

The tourists had begun to arrive in force earlier in the week, and their numbers would only swell as Halloween approached. But tonight was quiet; tourists usually stayed downtown, flocking to places where they could spend money, whether on a restaurant or a psychic reading, on a walking tour or a haunted house, so Gallows Hill would be empty, or nearly so. A silent twilight had spread out over the hill and the fields as he arrived.

There she was, as if waiting for him. The woman in white.

She stood by a small pile of tokens and gifts that had been left at the site over the past week—flowers and little white crosses, pentagrams and hand-written notes. The light from a white seven-day candle, beeswax in a glass cylinder, illuminated her serene features. She stood with her eyes closed. Her long white coat was buttoned to her throat and reached down to her ankles. She wore a broad-brimmed white hat, with white boots and a long ivory scarf. Lennox wondered how she managed to keep it all so spotlessly clean. The light from the candle made her blonde hair shine like dark gold. A quick glance showed no jewelry, no cross, no pentagram, nothing. No indication.

"Hello there," he said tentatively.

She opened her eyes and nodded. "Hello."

Silence.

"I understand that you've been coming out here each night since the police found that body."

"Yes" she said, taking her eyes from the candle and turning to face him. Her eyes were a soft gray. "I must."

"Why is that?"

"To burn the candle, to remember him, to hope that the police find his killer."

"Did you know him?" Lennox asked hopefully.

"No," she shook her head.

Damn, he thought.

"But he should be remembered," she said. "Taking a life is blasphemy; leaving the body here is desecration. It warrants a punishment beyond which any earthly justice can exact."

She turned back to the candle, and closed her gray eyes.

Lennox walked away, thinking that this strange woman was absolutely right.

Chapter VII

HE DRAGGED HIMSELF INTO THE STATION just after noon the next day, still weary from the night before. Ouellette stared at her computer screen, empty coffee mug next to her. The newspapers were already sitting on his desk, the Sudokus all done. The sleeves of her dark blue striped shirt were rolled up, topaz cufflinks sitting next to the mug. He smiled as he saw them—he had given her those cufflinks last year for her birthday. And while he knew her birthday, Ouellette remained characteristically silent about her actual age. He guessed she was a decade younger than him, so somewhere in her early thirties, but had never asked.

He had never met anyone quite like Michelle Ouellette outside the Coast Guard. She was very controlled, very driven, and she probably would have done well on the deck of a gale-tossed cutter. Glancing back and forth between their desks, Lennox decided that really, she had the neatest desk in the bullpen. Her deadpan was famous throughout the department. Several years ago, a badly decomposed body had been fished out of Salem Harbor; one senior detective had fainted while another ran off to vomit in the bushes, leaving Ouellette to process the scene by herself. Lennox had always admired her detachment, her ability to maintain a certain distance and regard the people and elements of an investigation as puzzle pieces. It was a trick he had never quite mastered.

She kept her personal life to herself. The only personal items on her neat desk were a small Canadian flag and a photo of Roland, her eight-year-old son. In all the time he had been partnered with her, the unmarried and resolutely single Ouellette had never once said a word about the boy's father, and his identity remained a topic of hushed speculation—speculation Lennox refused to take part in, especially when he heard that he himself had been considered a likely suspect.

"Heard it was a lively meeting last night," she said.

"Don't... want to talk about it," he replied.

"I got a hit on Mather's car in NCIC," she said, handing him a printout. "Found Tuesday morning in Beverly, in a supermarket parking lot." Beverly was the next town over. "It was a rental from a company in Boston, rented last Thursday."

"So he flew into Logan, rented a car, and drove to the Hawthorne," Lennox nodded. "If they found the car Tuesday, why are we only hearing about it now?"

"Store manager called it in Tuesday afternoon. Car had been sitting in his lot since Monday morning. Officer came out to have a look, but once he arrived on scene another call came in for a crime in progress, a convenience store robbery. Responding to that call, he broke an ankle."

"You're kidding."

"Between the robbery and the officer down, the abandoned car got lost in the shuffle for another day until the store manager called in to complain again yesterday. They sent someone else out and it got entered."

"Did they get the guy who knocked over the convenience store?" Lennox chuckled.

"They did."

"Well, that's good at least. So we have a body in Salem and a car in Beverly. Did he drive over there to meet someone? Someone who killed him and dumped the body back here?"

"Supermarket parking lot is a pretty public place to meet your murderer," Ouellette said thoughtfully.

"Maybe that's the point—he doesn't trust whoever it is, so meets them in a public place."

"Could be. But why leave the car and dump the body?"

"Somehow seems more likely they're both dumped. Which means the parking lot isn't the murder scene. But stringing up a body at Gallows Hill is all very... theatrical. Leaving a stolen car in a parking lot..." He shrugged. "Not so much. Do you know anyone over there? Beverly?"

"I do. Someone I used to know back when I was still in Mounted. I have a call in to him, asking to keep us informed. I sent Dworaczyk and Johnson over to check out the car and see if there's anything to be found. I'll let the Beverly PD sort things out with the rental company."

"What do you think of Harker's suggestion? That this is some crazy revenge killing for Cotton Mather and the witch trials?"

"Possible, but doesn't seem likely."

"Magnus Moon was at the meeting last night. He's crazy."

"He's eccentric," Ouellette said. "And harmless."

"We hope."

"Where do we stand on this case?" Lieutenant Winters asked. Lennox hadn't heard him coming. Again.

"We've identified the victim as a Mr. Paul Mather of Columbus, Ohio," Ouellette said. "An accountant, widower. We checked at the bank owned by the company he worked for and no one over there admits to seeing him or knowing anything. We have a call in to his sister, but haven't heard anything from her yet."

"You need to find something on this," Winters warned.

The old cliché about needing a solid lead within the first forty-eight hours of an investigation was, unfortunately, often true. The longer a case dragged on, the less likely it became that it could ever be closed. Annalisa Paiva's case, still open six years after her murder, was a particularly stark example.

"And Detective Lennox. Nice of you to join us today. I heard you chatted with the mayor last night after the crime watch meeting."

"Yeah..."

"He impressed upon you the gravity of our situation?"

"Oh, he did that."

"I'm authorizing overtime, additional manpower, whatever you need. Hell, you need the state police, the FBI, SEAL Team Six, whatever, I'll get it for you. Just close this damn case."

Ouellette nodded.

Turning back to Lennox, the Lieutenant asked pointedly, "And how is Paiva coming?"

Lennox opened his mouth to reply but Winters was already stalking away across the bullpen in silence.

"Do you need me?" Lennox asked, checking his watch.

"Not much to do until Dworaczyk and Johnson report in."

"I have a… thing."

"Go," Ouellette said. "I'll let you know when I hear something."

"Thanks."

He had arranged to meet Katherine in a coffee shop twenty minutes away in Marblehead. It had been one of the places he'd tried when out on his administrative leave, but soon decided that he liked neither the coffee nor the hipster ambiance of the place and stopped going after only a few visits. So he was not a familiar face here, which is what he wanted, and this was a meeting that could not possibly take place in Salem.

The place was packed with slackers hunched over laptops. The music was too loud and the lighting too low, more reasons he had stopped going. Katherine sat at a back table, thin hands wrapped around a bright ceramic mug with a chipped handle. She looked a little more relaxed than the last time he had seen her. A little. She may have been able to put some weight back on, he thought, but she was still too skinny, too sick-looking. She needed sleep and a shower and a change of clothes. She still looked like a junkie.

He bought a bottle of water and at down across from her.

"Chief," she nodded.

"At ease. Everything okay?"

She shrugged. "I was gonna ask you that."

"Everything's fine. They didn't bring charges, so I'm clear. I'm back to work. My report is filed and approved, and your name's not in there anywhere."

"Thanks, Andrew."

"Don't mention it," he said. "And I mean that—please don't ever mention it," he added with a dry laugh.

She managed a wan smile.

"I really appreciate it," she said. "I mean, things have just been so screwed up, and all I'd need is something like this…"

"Like I said, don't mention it. Are you in a program?"

"I'm wait-listed in, like, three places."

"I'll make some calls. There's a place in Boston we can probably get you into."

"Thanks."

"Yeah. Well, I can't really stay, so…"

"Look, before you go…"

She had a too-familiar look in her eyes. That hungry look.

"I can't give you money, Kathy," he said. "I've told you that before."

"I'm not gonna use it to get high."

"Yes, you are," he said. "You might not want to, but you will."

"Chief, please."

"No. Look, I have to go." He rose and stood there awkwardly, looking for something to say. All he could come up with was "Semper P."

It had sounded better in his head.

"Yeah," she said, giving him a weak salute. "Semper fucking P."

Outside, he washed down a Xanax with the last of the bottled water. Popping a pill after visiting a not-so-recovering addict. It made him feel awful.

It was his last pill, he realized. With the last week being what it had been, he hadn't even thought about refilling the prescription. He drove to the Walgreens on Boston Street, not far from

Gallows Hill Park, but far enough from the station that he was less likely to run into anyone here. He hoped.

A couple of brown brick tenement buildings stood near the store. They reminded him of the buildings along Ward Street, which in turn reminded him of how little progress he was making on closing the Paiva case.

There was a line at the pharmacy, and he submitted his slip and waited, paging distractedly though the old magazines piled up in the waiting area. Hurry-up-and-wait.

"Can't you get him on the phone?" an old man demanded too loudly.

"I haven't been able to," the young pharmacist said. In her too-large white lab coat, she looked like she had graduated pharmacy school about ten minutes ago. "And you have no more refills left on this—"

"You get him on the damn phone right now. I need my pills."

"Keep your voice down," the man's wife admonished.

"How long is it gonna take to fill my scrip?" someone else asked.

Lennox needed an anti-anxiety med twice as much now.

My God, is this it? he wondered. Would he be living out this little scene once a month for the rest of his life? Was he doomed to be one more person standing in line and waiting for the few milligrams of chemicals to get through the day? And wasn't Xanax addictive? He tried to be careful with it, but… he still shuddered at the thought.

Twenty minutes later, prescription filled, he sat in his car in the parking lot, staring at the small wooded hill that rose anonymously behind the store. This, he knew, was the site several modern historians argued was the real Gallows Hill. It fit the few contemporary descriptions and, in 1692, would have been just outside town limits, where Puritans tended to hold their executions. But Gallows Hill Park had over a century of oral tradition to uphold its claim, and in Salem, it was always the story that mattered.

He pulled out onto Proctor Street, named for John Proctor, hanged at Gallows Hill—wherever it was—and immortalized in

The Crucible. Here in Salem, he thought, we hang innocents and then, three centuries later, name streets after them and call it even.

His phone was ringing as he got back to the bullpen.

"Is this Detective Lennox?" a woman's voice asked nervously. "It's—it's Danielle Mather. You called about my brother? About Paul?"

He'd forgotten how much he was dreading this call. Notifying family of a murder was bad enough in person; doing it over the phone was immeasurably worse.

"Hi, Danielle," he said awkwardly. "Thanks for getting back to me. Yeah, we found Paul here in town on Monday morning, and I'm sorry to have to tell you, but thee's really no easy way to do this. He was dead when we found him."

"What?" her voice rose. "That can't be right. It can't be Paul."

"It's him, ma'am. I'm sorry."

"What happened?"

"That's what we're trying to figure out now."

"I don't understand..."

"It looks like a homicide," he said. How much should he tell her? Your brother was found hanging from a tree, with pentagrams on his palms and his head knocked in... Lennox wanted to bang his head on his desk. "What was he doing here in Salem? Did he know people here?"

He'd checked the phone listings and hadn't found a Mather family anywhere for miles.

"No... He was... he was looking for his birth parents."

"Birth parents? Wait—he was adopted?"

"Yes," she replied hesitantly. "My parents wanted another child and they went to an adoption agency. But... we grew up like brother and sister."

"Wait—I'm here with my partner, Sergeant Ouellette. Let me put you on speaker, okay? So, he was looking for his birth parents. Was he able to find them?"

"Yes and no. He found records on his mother, his birth mother. She was a single mother at… what was the place called? Danvers State Hospital."

Lennox closed his eyes. Danvers State was a psychiatric hospital. It was infamous.

"His birth name was Charles Christopher Musgrave," Danielle went on. "His mother was named Patience, I think."

"You are kidding me," Lennox said. "Musgrave?"

"Why?" she asked. "Does that mean something?"

"Oh, yeah. Does it ever. Do you know if he got in touch with them?"

"I… I don't. He said he'd go to Salem and then… decide."

"Was there anything else?"

"There may have been a probate matter," she said quietly.

"An inheritance?"

"Possibly. Probate matters are filed at City Hall, and I know that was supposed to be his first stop when he arrived in town. Before reaching out to the Musgrave family."

"Were you in touch with him when he was here in town?"

"No."

"Not at all?"

"No. Not at all. He was going to touch base with me on Monday. But…"

"Okay. The medical examiner will get in touch with you about getting the body… about getting him back home to you." He had no idea what else he could say to her.

"Okay," she said quietly.

"Ma'am," Ouellette said, "we're going to work very hard to find out what happened. We'll be in touch the minute we find out anything, all right?"

"All right…"

"So he's not descended from Cotton Mather," Lennox said, hanging up the phone. "He's descended from Silas Musgrave."

"And who is that?" Ouellette asked.

"Seriously? You don't know the story?"

"Seriously, I don't know the story."

"It was a dark and stormy night," Lennox began.

"Knock it *off*."

"Okay, so Silas Musgrave was among the first group of settlers to arrive with Roger Conant back in 1626. He has his wife and children with him. He was, from all accounts, not a nice man. He's a mean, tight-fisted old sinner. During the witch trials, he cries out on a wealthy neighbor, and gets him sent to Gallows Hill."

"And the accuser usually got the accused's property."

"Right. And Silas builds a new mansion on the land he stole—they say he started building before the neighbor's body was even cut down. Then he seems to decide that getting people hanged is fun, and he starts to testify against others. When Cotton Mather comes to town to oversee things, Silas lends him the Musgrave family Bible, brought over from England, to preach from.

"Eventually, his wife and children leave and Silas lives alone in that big old house and dark rumors swirl. They say he's practicing black magic and despoiling local virgins."

"So why didn't anyone cry out on him?"

"Don't know. Maybe no one dared. But a few years after the witch trials are over, Silas's house, built on that stolen land, is struck by lightning and burns to the ground. The only thing that survives?"

"The Bible."

"A sure sign of God's judgment upon Silas for his wicked, wicked ways," Lennox nodded. "Children grow up and they aren't much better than him—they go into whaling and slave trading and what have you, and eventually build another house on that land around 1800. It's a McIntire house. It's still there."

"Family still live there?"

"Oh, yes. And apparently they're still all dark and weird. Kids cross the street so they don't have to walk in front of the house. A couple of years ago, I saw a woman walking her dog, a big German shepherd, and the dog was barking at the house, pulling at the leash. I thought he was going to pull the poor woman over. And the dog wasn't being aggressive—it was terrified."

"And how do you know all this, exactly?" Ouellette asked as he finished his story.

"How can you live here and not know all this?"

"Fine. So he was here looking for family after all."

"He was here looking for the weirdest family in town," Lennox muttered. "Which is saying something."

"True."

"Okay, Sergeant, I'm ready to talk to them when you are."

"You're driving," she said.

Chapter VIII

THE MUSGRAVE MANSION looked like a haunted house.

It loomed at the end of a narrow street, a three-story brick edifice standing head and shoulders above the other houses. Half the families in Salem would have killed for a Samuel McIntire house; working under the patronage of the wealthy Derby family, McIntire was the celebrated architect and carver who had created many of the city's stately Federal style buildings and homes. And the Musgrave mansion was a textbook example of Federal architecture—from the fanlight and classical columns around the door, to the symmetrical rows of six-over-six windows; the windows on the third floor, the servants' quarters, were smaller. Huge brick chimneys swept upward at either end of the building. A decorative balustrade crowned the hip roof. It was an impressive building.

Standing on the sidewalk, Lennox looked up at the house. An architect might have said that the house's massing was too strong, its lines too aggressive, its decorative detailing too heavy. To Lennox, the building simply looked *off* somehow, intimidating, almost angry, as though Salem's premiere architect had designed the Musgrave mansion on a very bad day.

The autumn sunset threw orange shadows across the brick façade as Lennox and Ouellette approached. He could smell woodsmoke, and thin white wisps curled from one chimney. They nodded to one another and Lennox knocked on the front door using the huge knocker, a scowling lion's head with a brass ring in its mouth. He imagined the sound echoing down dark corridors within. They waited on the step uneasily.

After a long moment, the door opened a crack and a woman peered out. "Yes?"

"Ma'am, I'm Detective Lennox and this is Sergeant Ouellette. We need to ask you a few questions. Do you mind if we come in?"

He had delivered some form of this little speech a hundred times during his seven years as a detective, and yet he never did so without a slight tightening of the throat, a certain nervous sense that things were about to change and they almost always changed for the worse. Even the thought of speaking those too-familiar words made him uncomfortable.

"Oh," the woman said, hauling the heavy door open wide. Lennox half-expected it to groan dramatically on its hinges, and was almost disappointed when it didn't. She glanced back over her shoulder uncertainly before saying, "Yes, of course, come in."

She was slender and well-dressed in a casually expensive way, and probably older than she looked at first glance; Lennox guessed she might be ten years older than he was. She had a long square face with a strong jaw, firm but still attractive, and her pale blonde hair hung to her shoulders. As she shut the door behind them, he realized just how closely she resembled the dead man. A family resemblance, without a doubt.

"I'm Laura," she said.

"You live here?"

"I grew up here; Musgrave is my maiden name."

"And now it's…?"

"Gagnon," she replied.

The front hall was lofty and airy, with the dying sun streaming in through the long windows. There was a thick colorful Turkish carpet and candle sconces and long-faced portraits on the pale paneled walls. Not at all the brooding Gothic interior that Lennox had imagined.

Laura led them to a parlor off the front hall. The wide floorboards creaked as they entered the room.

The parlor was dominated by a giant portrait hanging over the mantel of the grand fireplace where a low fire smoldered and crackled. The dour visage of Silas Musgrave stared down with flinty disapproval, a nasty glint in his eye. Under one arm was the great family Bible, clutched to him as an outward show of piety, and his other hand rested on the hilt of a sword. With grizzled hair flowing over his shoulders and a crimson sash across his chest, he looked like some dissolute swashbuckler, with a cruel mouth and a lantern jaw. The portrait commanded Lennox's attention upon entering, and his eyes went there before he even noticed the two people beneath it.

Sitting by the fire was a woman who looked older than the house. She occupied a high-backed wooden wheelchair, another antique, with a worn and faded plaid blanket tucked around her legs. She had a narrow, craggy face with a beak of a nose and a mouth with a harsh curl, the face of a Halloween witch. She wore her long white hair in a heavy braid like a hangman's rope. She turned to the detectives as they came into the room. Her eyes were ice blue and her expression was every bit as disapproving as the old Puritan over the mantel. She licked dry lips and took a long puff on a briarwood pipe and blue-black smoke gathered around her. Lennox could smell it from across the room. In his experience, even nonsmokers liked the smell of pipe tobacco, but whatever the old woman was smoking was just foul.

Across from her, deep in a leather armchair, was a middle-aged man in khakis and a shapeless sweater. He rose slowly to his feet and, with a glance at the old woman, also turned to regard the newcomers with suspicion. His gaze lingered on Ouellette as he looked them both up and down. He had a black eye, a purple stain under his left eye. Lennox could tell the man had once been athletic, and probably not all that long ago.

The deep, faded curtains were drawn against the sunset, and several antique floor lamps, Tiffany originals by the look of them, lit the chamber dimly. The curtains and the smoldering fire kept the pleasant autumn locked outside, and somehow made the high-ceilinged room cramped and claustrophobic, feeling smaller than it actually was. The walls were painted in a deep yellow more sickly than bright, and the floorboards were wider than Lennox's foot was long. Usually, you had to pay admission to enter a house like this, he thought, while a docent toured you through the rooms.

Lennox glanced at the old photographs on the walls—gray and sepia pictures of old Salem, of sights long gone. Shelves held elegantly tarnished heirloom silver plate. But across the room, a pair of silver candlesticks on a little Queen Anne table caught his eye. They were simple and smooth and the only silver in the room not blurred and patinaed with age; they had been polished. Recently. His throat tightened as he wondered how neatly the bases of those heavy antiques would fit the depressed fractures in Paul Mather's skull.

"This is my mother, Agatha Musgrave," Laura said. "And my brother, Benedict."

Lennox nodded. Benedict had the same rangy build, the same long jaw as Laura, but she wore the family resemblance much better than he did.

"What do you want?" Agatha asked, as Laura took a few steps away. The old woman's voice was pure New England patrician, part ice water, part vinegar, all disapproval.

"We're investigating the death of a Mr. Paul Mather," Ouellette said, badge in hand. "You may have read about it in the paper. His body was found on Monday."

"I don't read the newspapers," Agatha said dismissively.

"We have reason to believe he may have tried to contact you last week."

"No one tried to contact me last week. What did you say the name was?"

"Paul Mather," Lennox said.

"I have never heard of him."

"Our information indicates he may have been the son of a Patience Musgrave," Lennox said. "Who is she?"

"What information is that?" Benedict asked.

"Information we've obtained in the course of our investigation," Ouellette said before Lennox could.

"Patience was my daughter," Agatha said slowly. "She was... troubled. She did not live up to the Musgrave name. Eventually, she went to Danvers State Hospital. She died soon after."

"She had a child while she was there."

"I told you. She was troubled."

"We think the man we found on Monday may be Patience's child," Ouellette said. "We think he came here looking for you, for your family."

"No such person came to this house," the old woman said sourly. "If he had, and if he was who you say he was, he would not have been welcome here. Patience was no Musgrave, and neither was her bastard child, wherever it might be. Benedict, my medicine."

Lennox noticed Laura had retreated to a far corner. She stood with her arms folded tightly around her, staring at the floor.

"Detectives," Benedict said, stepping forward, placing himself between them and Constance. "My sister Patience is a painful subject for the family and frankly, none of your business. You've upset my mother. We can't be of any help to you, and we'd like you to leave."

"Do you live here?" Lennox asked.

"Yes, I do," Benedict blinked, seemingly surprised they were not going. People must seldom have disobeyed Agatha. "Down the hall."

"But you don't," he said, turning to Laura. "You said you grew up here—so you don't live her now?"

"No." She gave him an address in a pricey condo complex, down by the water.

"Did Paul Mather try to contact you?"

"No," Laura said in a small voice.

"Detectives, now that you've dragged out the dirty laundry, I really think you should go." Benedict said.

"If you can think of anything, please let us know," Ouellette said, leaving her card on a small Queen Anne tea table. Lennox added his. They had no doubt the cards would be tossed into the fire as soon as the front door closed behind them.

"Yes, of course."

"Benedict," the old woman said impatiently.

Benedict silently steered Ouellette and Lennox out of the house and into the street, slamming the big front door shut. They heard a bolt groaning slowly into place.

The figure of Laura Gagnon appeared briefly at the parlor's window. She slowly drew the curtains.

"That went well," Lennox said.

"*Ferme ta gueule*," Ouellette allowed herself a tight grin.

"Benedict," Lennox said.

"What about him?"

"He was at the park the day we found the body."

"You're sure?"

"I never forget a face. He was hanging back in the crowd, off to the left. But he was there. It was him. And did you notice the rugs?"

"Rugs in the hall, and in the other two rooms off the hall that I noticed," she nodded.

"But not in the parlor where they receive their guests. Like they got rid of it. And did you see the silver candlesticks on the table? They were the only pieces of silver in that room that had been polished in the last hundred years– they were *gleaming*. They'd been cleaned recently. Had to get the blood off."

"This is our murder scene," Ouellette said, looking up at the house.

"Yes, it is," he agreed. "Not enough for a warrant, though."

"Not yet," she corrected.

Across the street, a college age kid in a top hat and swirling black cape stood before a knot of a dozen tourists, pointing up at the house with his ebony cane. A walking tour. October in Salem. Lennox crossed the street, motioning for Ouellette to follow him.

"...a sure sign of God's wrath upon Silas for his wicked misdeeds," the kid intoned in a too-deep voice, attempting an English accent, but only sounding like he had a mouthful of marbles. "Subsequent generations of the family have sought to rehabilitate the family legacy. In the 1890s, the Reverend Doctor John Musgrave, living *in this very house*, became a noted theologian and collector of Biblical texts. Reverend Doctor Musgrave amassed over a dozen different rare historic editions, having an especial fondness for misprints. In his collection is the so-called Murderer's Bible from 1801, wherein the printer had put *Murderer* where it should read *Murmurer*, so Jude 16 reads, *These are murderers, complainers, walking after their own lusts; and their mouth speaketh great swelling words.*"

This got an anemic chuckle from the crowd.

The kid noticed the detectives standing nearby.

"This is a nightly haunted history walking tour offered by Salem Witch Trails," he said, holding up a warning hand in a fingerless glove. "We depart every evening at seven o'clock from in front of the visitor center. Tickets must be purchased in advance—"

"We're cops," Lennox said, showing his badge.

"Oh, shit," the kid said, accent suddenly gone. "Sorry, dude. I mean, officer. Look, my boss is like totally licensed, and I just do the tours so I don't know—"

"Yeah, okay, fine. Did you do tours last weekend?"

"Yeah. Thursday, Friday, and Saturday."

"Did you by any chance see this guy on any of those nights?" Lennox asked, pulling the photo of Paul Mather from his organizer.

The kid squinted in the twilight.

"Um, maybe? Friday night, while I was doing the spiel, a guy came out of that house, which kinda freaked the shit outta me because no one ever comes out of that house, you know?"

"Was it him?"

"I dunno. Coulda been. It was dark. A guy came out of the house and a woman was standing inside the door when he left. I noticed her more than him, you know? She was kinda hot for an older chick. Blonde. I like blondes," he shrugged.

"What time?" Ouellette asked.

"It'd be now," the kid said. "Like seven-thirty, seven-forty. That's when I get here."

"Okay, thanks."

The kid awkwardly moved the tour on to its next spot, leaving the detectives there on the sidewalk opposite the Musgrave mansion. Lennox was convinced that the jack-o-lanterns leering from front steps and picture windows up and down the street were, in fact, laughing at them both.

Chapter IX

LENNOX ARRIVED AT THE STATION the next morning to find that Ouellette had moved the investigation into the Major Case Room, off the bullpen. There was a large conference table, whiteboards and cork bulletin boards now arrayed with notes and crime scene photos. The dead man stared back at them twice, once from his DMV picture, and once from the morgue photo—once alive, once dead. There was a computer in one corner of the room, where Ouellette now sat, and a monitor that was linked to the two interview rooms on the first floor.

The Major Case Room was mostly used for storage, and a stack of boxes teetered dangerously at one end, old cases and half-forgotten records. Lennox was fairly certain no one knew exactly what was in them. The last time he had been in the room was six months ago, when Patrolman Shoemaker had been promoted to detective, and half a dozen pizza boxes had been arranged along the table. He thought he could still catch the faint whiff of anchovy, but that was probably just in his head.

"Benedict Musgrave has a record," Ouellette said, looking up from the NCIC screen.

"Oh, really?"

"Assault. And he has a restraining order on him."

"Do tell."

"Two years ago, assault on one James Carson. According to the report, Carson 'stole' his fiancée, one Amanda Lewis."

"Someone was going to marry into that family?" Lennox chuckled.

"She evidently changed her mind, smart girl. And when she did, Benedict naturally went after the new man."

"A history of violence. This family gets better and better. Do we have an address on the happy couple?"

"We do," Ouellette said.

"I think I'd like to get a character reference on Benedict."

"You're driving."

Mr. and Mrs. James Carson lived in a moderately nice house in a quiet neighborhood. Picket fence, two cars, a dog, and unhappy memories of Benedict Musgrave.

"Guy needs serious help," Jim Carson said.

"You two were dating?" Ouellette turned to Amanda.

"Yes…" she began hesitantly. She sat on the far end of a leather couch with her hands folded tightly in her lap. "I know it's probably hard to believe, but he can actually be quite charming."

"But…?"

"But he changed, and—I'm sorry. Why are you asking about this? I haven't seen or heard from him in a couple of years."

"It's routine to check up periodically in cases where a restraining order has been issued," Lennox lied. "So there's been no contact?"

"No."

"Not easy in a small city like this," he smiled.

"Easier than you'd think, really."

"You were saying that he'd changed?" Ouellette prodded.

"Yes. It was nice for a while. He was all very eighteenth century about things—he seemed to think that giving me the Musgrave name was going to be quite the honor."

"But?"

"But the family was broke. Not that that mattered to me, but it mattered to him. They'd made their money years ago in shipping—whaling and slaving, mostly. But they lost nearly everything in 1914, in the fire."

In June of 1914, after a long drought, a fire broke out in the factory district along Boston Street, engulfing much of downtown. Thousands lost their homes and their livelihood as the blaze soon gutted the city. It was said that the flames could be seen as far away as Boston, and the wreckage smoldered for days. Salem was slow to recover. Lennox remembered hearing somewhere that the ghost of Giles Corey, the man pressed to death for refusing to recognize the authority of the Court of Oyer and Terminer during the witch trials, was supposedly seen just before the fire broke out. According to legend, Corey's ghost was a harbinger of doom.

"The living room of their house is decorated with pictures of the buildings they used to own," she said.

Lennox remembered seeing several such photos yesterday when interviewing the family.

"They're all gone now, they burnt. Except for one. There was a brick mill building the family owned, and Benedict was negotiating with a developer who wanted it for condos. Supposedly, there were all kinds of tunnels and hidden rooms in the place, going back to some ancestor, a bootlegger or a slave trader, I forget now. He thought that the money was going to help the family get back on its feet, and then we could get married. But the soil turned out to be contaminated—lead and creosote and God knows what else, all left over from the fire. So the deal fell through and he was stuck with an empty old mill he couldn't do anything with. He always said that fire was the Musgrave family curse, going back to old Silas."

"You two split up after the mill went south?"

"Yes, but it's not like that. Before I met him, he'd studied law but couldn't pass the bar, so he was bitter about that. And then when the mill deal fell through, he… changed. He was really hoping this was going to turn things around and when it fell apart, he became very depressed, very angry. Scary. He just retreated, and spent his time locked up in that old mansion reading… reading true crime books," she laughed uncomfortably. "Stuff about serial killers. He was always a little morbid."

"And then you split up."

"I met Jim, and told Benny I was leaving."

"And that's when he came after me," James Carson said. "Broke my nose, saying I stole Mandy. Crazy bastard."

"And you haven't seen him since?"

"God no," Jim said, running a finger over the bridge of his nose. "Crazy bastard has issues. And he'll really have issues if he ever shows up here."

Salem Jail opened in 1813, a grim granite house of correction and contrition that frowned out over a historic graveyard. The hundred cells had housed any number of malefactors over the years, including Albert deSalvo, the Boston Strangler, after being arrested in neighboring Lynn. The prison yard had seen over fifty executions—all hangings, Salem's preferred method of punishment, apparently. The jail remained in use for a hundred and seventy-eight years, when it was closed down and stood empty and decaying, plagued by vandals and trespassers. Rehabbed by a developer and renamed 50 St. Peter Street for its address, an attempt to gloss over the building's origins, it had opened as an apartment complex a few years ago.

Lennox had lived in the old jail since the divorce. He had needed to find a place that could be his, that had never been theirs, fraught with once-happy memories mocking him from every corner. The fact that the only available apartment in his price range was one of the smaller ones in the old jail was a weird slap in the face. The jail had been shut down years before he'd even joined the force; he'd still been in the Coast Guard, doing safety inspections and pulling foundering boats off the rocks. So at least he didn't have to live in the same place where he'd once locked up suspects.

His apartment was sparsely furnished, almost austere. This was less an aesthetic and more a lack of effort. He lived like some kind of strange monk. Not owning a TV, he was spared the horror of seeing coverage of Thursday's crime watch meeting on the news. He was sure it must be playing in an endless loop somewhere. A rack of CDs reached up one exposed brick wall, and a packed bookcase covered the other. Both sets of shelves were more-or-less alphabetized. He liked to think that this was leftover Coastie discipline, but he had to make a conscious effort to put the books and discs back where they belonged.

He unfolded himself on the couch, feeling the knots in his back and his legs pop uncomfortably, and watched the shadows lengthen as the sun set.

This had been the worst week he'd had in a long, long time. He was pretty sure that Winters, never an admirer, now actually hated him. It had taken a week to find a solid lead on the case, and he almost certainly looked foolish in the news footage, no doubt inspiring serious questions about the department's ability to handle the case. Great. He was a one-man PR disaster. At least he hadn't shot anyone this week. He tucked a Xanax under his tongue and let it slowly dissolve into a chalky bitterness that matched his mood.

On the edge of the coffee table sat a silver cigarette case, sleek art deco, with his initials engraved in smooth copperplate, *ADL*. A birthday present from Ellen, back when they were first dating. It had taken her months of searching, she said, to find an antique case with the right initials. He picked it up now, running his fingers over the monogram and wondering, once again, who the other, long-gone *ADL* had been. He'd always loved the gift; it showed how thoughtful and how thorough Ellen could be. But now, it only served as a relic of parts of his life that were gone. His smoking, his marriage…

He closed his eyes… and he stood atop a bare and windswept Gallows Hill, where the accused met their God at the end of a rope. He faced a crowd—a mob. The Musgraves were there, skulking in the back, Agatha with a scowl and Benedict with smugly folded arms. Nearby, the Paivas, Gloria and Estacio, looked sorry for him. Behind them, hazy in the distance, sharp roofs of old Salem jutted up through a wintry fog.

Paul Mather and Annalisa Paiva stood apart from the crowd, regarding him sadly. He realized they were holding hands.

Winters, swathed in rusty black with a curly Puritan wig

and buckle shoes, glowered at him from astride a white charger.

"What say you?" Winters demanded.

And Lennox felt a noose tighten around his throat.

One chance, he thought desperately. One chance only, one chance to get it right.

"You have the right to remain silent," he recited. Slowly. Calmly. He couldn't afford a single mistake, a single mumbled word or slurred phrase. "Anything you say can and will be used against you in a court of law. You have the right to an attorney. If you cannot afford an attorney one will be provided for you. Do you understand these rights as I have read them to you?"

Perfect.

The crowd gathered on the hilltop looked to Winters.

"The Black Man whispers to him!" someone cried. "I see it!"

"Hang him!" someone called.

"Let him hang!" yelled someone else.

"The Devil oft hath been transformed into an angel of light," Winters shouted. "Hang the man!"

No, wait… they couldn't hang him if he recited it perfectly. He knew they couldn't. It was a test…

Dworaczyk jerked away the ladder upon which Lennox balanced. The crowd howled, shrieked, crying out…

He snapped awake, gasping for breath.

It wasn't a howling crowd, it was his cell phone.

"Lennox," he mumbled.

"I need you at the station." Ouellette's voice. "Someone just got caught trying to break into the Musgrave house."

"I'll be right there," he said groggily. He set down the phone and raised his hand absently to his throat, not quite sure what he was checking for. Reaching for his coat, he realized he still had the silver cigarette case in the other hand, sleek art deco, cold and hard.

"What the hell happened?" Lennox asked when he arrived at the station.

Ouellette was in the Major Case Room. The anchovy smell still hadn't gone away. She nodded toward the monitor showing a hollow-cheeked man downstairs in Interrogation Room Two. Leather jacket over a hoodie, shaven head, spiky tribal neck tattoos.

"Meet Mr. Eric Scully," she said. "Attempted B&E on the Musgrave mansion an hour ago."

"Who is he?"

"From Dorchester. Priors for Assault, B&E, Disorderly Conduct, the usual petty criminal resume." She waved a printout. "A neighbor saw him working on a window from across the street and called it in; there was a cruiser a few streets away."

"The neighbor didn't happen to see our victim a few nights ago?" Lennox asked hopefully.

Ouellette shook her head.

"Of course not," he said. "What does have to say for himself?"

"He's not saying anything."

"What does the family say?"

"They aren't answering the door. Uniforms knocked, and the lights in the house went out one by one."

On the monitor, Eric Scully looked up at the camera mounted in the far corner of the interrogation room's ceiling, glowering. He threw his arms wide in an angry shrug.

"Impatient," Lennox murmured.

"I was letting him stew for a while before sending in Dworaczyk to question him."

"Looks like he's ready."

"Agreed." She swiped at her smartphone's screen and said, "Okay, go."

They watched as Dworaczyk entered the interrogation room and sat across from Eric Scully. He slapped a legal pad down and rapped his knuckles on the plastic tabletop.

"So, Eric, we have a witness who saw you sneaking around that house, and then our witness saw you starting to work on one of the windows, like you were trying to open it. Those old windows must be a bitch, huh? So we definitely have you on that. So what the hell were you doing?"

"Lawyer."

"You do not want a lawyer getting mixed up in all this," Dworaczyk said quietly. "You and I, we can sort this out by ourselves. But if a lawyer gets in the middle of it, forget it. No chance of getting this thing cleared up. Now, why were you trying to break into that house tonight, Eric?"

"I want my lawyer, now."

"At this point, a lawyer really will not be much help to you. We have a witness who saw you engaging in criminal activity, and you have a criminal record, Eric. A pretty long criminal record, actually. Do you really think a lawyer can help you here? Because I, for one, do not. I can help you, not some lawyer. So you know those people in the house?"

"I want my lawyer. Right the fuck *now*."

"And I am telling you, your best bet here is to talk to us, tell us what you were doing, why you were trying to break into this particular house. Because then, then—"

There was a curt knock on the door, and a uniform brought a tall man in a dark suit into frame on the monitor.

"I'm Mr. Scully's legal representative," the man said, face turned very much away from the camera. "My client will not be answering any questions, detective, and I want that camera off while I confer with my client."

"See you in hell, pal," Dworaczyk said to both of them, slamming the door shut as he went.

"Lawyer's name is Johanssen," Dworaczyk said, coming into the Major Case Room and flipping a business card onto the table.

Lennox ran a finger across the embossed lettering. Essex Partners was a well-known on the North Shore.

"What's a guy with neck tattoos doing with an actual lawyer from an actual law firm?" he asked.

"Damned if I know," Dworaczyk shrugged. "Where to from here, Michelle?"

"Book him for attempted breaking and entering," she said quietly. Lennox could tell she was unhappy about it. "All we can do right now."

Dworaczyk slammed the door again as he left the room, going back downstairs to process Scully.

"So that went well," Lennox said.

"Shut up."

"Assuming this isn't just a coincidence—"

"That would be asking too much," she said.

"Right. Assuming this isn't just a coincidence, just a B&E, what do we think Scully was up to?"

"He wasn't carrying," she said. "All he had was a small crowbar in a messenger bag. I don't think he was looking for anyone in the house."

"Or at least not looking to hurt anyone in the house, but then again, a crowbar would work fine if he had to. Dammit."

"What?"

"This guy probably knows more about what's going on than we do," Lennox rubbed his eyes. "I think I'm starting to really hate this case."

Chapter X

SUNDAY MORNINGS WERE QUIET IN SALEM, even during October. When there was no case to work, and there often wasn't, Lennox could start the day with breakfast and a slow stroll around town, people watching, and then lazily reading some history book or other. He was almost used to spending his Sundays alone by now. Almost. Sometimes his daughter Allison joined him for lunch, or a movie, or a long walk. But their time together only underscored how little they actually saw one another now.

He knew his first stop on Monday morning was to be City Hall, only a few streets away from his apartment. He needed to see what was on file there, see what gaps those documents could fill in. But even if he couldn't make progress on the Musgrave case today, he still had a full day ahead of him.

Red's Sandwich Shop was a diner where locals had eaten for over fifty years. The place was always packed, and Lennox usually went in early to beat the crush of tourists. It occupied a plainspoken clapboard building that had been a landmark and a meeting place for some three centuries; the building had once been the London Coffee House, and borne silent witness to meetings of Salemites arguing about taxes and debating politics. Not much had changed on this Sunday morning, though now the restaurant was surrounded by fortunetellers, trolley tours, and pricey gift shops. He finished his omelet, and got a large coffee to go.

Most cops on the force had a second source of income. Two of them owned a bar together, and one was a silent partner in a pizza place. Many picked up extra work doing security. Five years ago, Lennox had opened the Black Museum, Salem's only true crime museum, on busy Derby Street downtown. Dioramas and scenes depicting some of history's most infamous criminals and their victims were on display for the edification and delight of tourists who paid the eight-dollar admission.

There were almost fifty displays in the museum. He commissioned work from various local artists to create the various scenes and life-sized figures. There was the obligatory section devoted to the witch trials—a crime if ever there was one, Lennox reasoned, even if he personally thought there had been no witches in Salem prior to 1970 or so—but the rest of the museum was given over to names and events both well-remembered and long-forgotten. A menacing Lizzie Borden, brandishing her ax, face spattered with blood, stood across from a top-hatted Jack the Ripper, his face half-hidden by a white silk scarf, making no attempt to hide the long knife in one hand. John White Webster, the Harvard chemist, was hard at work dismembering the body of Doctor George Parkman just steps away from Lizzie and Jack. Scott, the artist who had done half a dozen of the displays, had worked particularly hard on that display, casting Parkman's body parts in silicone and carefully mixing the blood to a particular opacity. In the alcove next to Webster, Reverend Ephraim Avery loomed murderously over the slight figure of Sarah Maria Cornell, the mill girl carrying his child. Cornell's body had been found hanging in a field of haystacks, and Lennox noted that the display needed fresh straw.

His favorite display was devoted to the murder of Joseph White, a tight-fisted old Yankee trader, a sea captain who amassed a fortune in the slave trade. In April, 1830, White had been found murdered, his skull fractured and his body stabbed over a dozen times, in the bed of his elegant Salem home. An ominous Committee of Vigilance investigated the crime and patrolled the streets, only ratcheting up already-feverish tensions. Richard and George Crowninshield, sons of an eminent and ancient family,

were soon arrested for the crime, along with their accused hench-
men, another pair of brothers, Joe and Frank Knapp. Joe Knapp
signed a confession, stating that while they had all conspired to
kill the old man, Richard Crowninshield was the murderer. The
gang had hoped to make off with the treasure in the iron chest at
the foot of White's bed—treasure which was not there when the
chest was broken open. Richard hanged himself in his cell, George
was cleared, and the Knapp brothers, found guilty in a trial elo-
quently prosecuted by Daniel Webster, were hanged in the prison
yard. Probably, Lennox mused grimly, right outside his window.

The case had made international headlines in its day; Nathaniel Hawthorne followed the trial, and Edgar Allan Poe almost
certainly did. White's house, now called the Gardner-Pingree
House and owned by the Peabody-Essex Museum, still stood on
Essex Street. It was included on half a dozen walking tours. Lennox
had haphazardly collected material on the case for years, more a
hobby than a serious pursuit. Some day, after he retired, he told
himself he would write a book.

Richard Crowninshield, a club in one hand and a dagger
in the other, scowled out from the alcove where he lurked. The
beady-eyed Knapp brothers hunched behind him, by the bloody
headboard. Yes, Lennox had always liked this display.

A few feet away was a display devoted to Salem's other
infamous crime, the unsolved murder of Frances Cochran. In a
sultry July of 1941, the nineteen-year-old Cochran's body—mu-
tilated, violated, set afire and with a tree branch shoved into her
throat—was found in some woods on the edge of town. She had
last been seen getting into a square-backed black car the night
before. Other police departments joined in the investigation that
spanned years; nearly two thousand witnesses were questioned,
suspects were arrested and later released, and at least twenty men
offered false confessions. Her killer was never found.

A nervous-looking Frances stood before a noir painted back-
drop of a streetlamp and a sinister, hulking car. She clutched her
purse in both hands. Lennox had always thought that her manikin

was probably the most realistic in the museum, and certainly the one most visitors stopped to sadly ponder as they made their way through the criminals gathered here.

The last display, near the exit, consisted of several sepia-toned photographs, each illustrating the various sins dubbed "The Crime of the Century"—the murder of Stanford White, Leopold and Loeb, the Lindbergh baby kidnapping, the Brinks robbery... where he drew the line. Lennox lost interest in historic crimes after about 1950 or so. OJ and Casey Anthony would have to go on without him. He was never quite sure what to do with the small, empty alcove at the far end of the room—sometimes he thought he should put up a small sign saying it was the Judge Crater display.

He spent an hour dusting and straightening, taking notes on the changes he needed to make. He wanted to change the lighting on this murderer, get a new coat for that victim. In the little gift shop, where he stocked mugs, T-shirts, and cheap local history books and lurid true crime paperbacks, he thought about what needed to be reordered and what should be put on clearance.

Lennox glanced at his watch; Adam, who manned the counter and sold tickets, should be in to open the museum for noon. Adam's father had designed the Frances Cochran figure.

He spent a few minutes in the back office, glancing over last year's numbers. There was a desiccated toothbrush in his desk drawer, a relic from the two-week period after the divorce, when he couldn't find an apartment and had slept on the couch here in the office. He'd kept expecting that desperate call—*wait, Drew, I was wrong, it was all a mistake, let's go home.* But the call never came.

He heard the front door open. Sunlight spilled into the darkened museum.

"Mr. Lennox? You here?"

Adam. He was a gangly kid in his twenties who usually wore clunky boots and gray turtlenecks, even in the summer. On slow days, he settled into the tall chair behind the counter and read a dog-eared paperback copy of *The House of the Seven Gables*. He'd worked for Lennox almost three years and had either never been able to finish the book, or had been reading and re-reading it all this time. Lennox never asked.

"I'm back here. How was it this week? I meant to check in but I was pretty busy."

"Yeah. I saw in the news that you're handling that guy they found over at Gallows Hill. How's that going?"

"No comment. How was it here this week?"

"Lotta French tourists. I need to learn French."

"I'll send Ouellette over."

"Had to throw some people out on Friday."

"Oh God," Lennox groaned. "What now?"

"Some dude was groping Lizzie Borden."

"You're kidding."

"Nope. His buddies were taking pictures with their phones. Threw 'em out, but the pictures went up on Facebook like an hour later."

One of his strengths as a detective, or so he thought, was that he genuinely liked people, and honestly tried to understand them. But since opening the Black Museum, Lennox realized that sometimes he didn't understand people at all.

"Okay, well, if something like that happens again," he shrugged. "…call the cops."

"Sure."

"You've got enough change in the register, and you should be all set. Vanessa's coming?"

Vanessa was Scott's daughter. She worked nights and weekends during the season.

"Yeah, she'll be in at one."

"Okay. Call me if you need anything."

"Okay, Mr. Lennox. See you."

He stepped outside into Derby Street, squinting in the sunlight. The tourists were just waking up and going in search of their breakfast. He needed another coffee, decaf, from the deli down the street. Right next to the parking garage where Antonio Ramirez worked, the man in the booth.

At the deli, he waited in line and got his coffee, picking up copies of the *Argus* and the *Advertiser*. Tucking them under one arm and putting too much sugar into his decaf, he turned and nearly spilled his coffee down Ed Fuller's shirt.

"Easy there, detective."

"Sorry, Ed. Good morning."

"What're you doing up this early?" Ed asked. Most locals tended to stay indoors, hunkered down, while their city was besieged by Halloween tourists.

"Work to do. The Paiva case. Going to talk to the boyfriend."

"Antonio?" Fuller asked, taking a moment to come up with the name. "The guilty party himself?"

"So you think he did it?" Lennox asked, lowering his voice.

"Seemed likely at the time. But Curwen couldn't place him at the scene, so..."

"You worked a few cases with him, right?"

"A few."

"I never did. Good cop?"

"Good cop," Fuller nodded. "He saw what was in front of him. But that kind of cuts both ways, you know?"

"Right. If it wasn't in front of him, Curwen didn't know about it?"

"Sometimes. And he wasn't always so... broad minded."

"Meaning?"

"He didn't always do so well with the people in the Point. Didn't have a lot of patience with anyone who wasn't born-and-bred local, didn't speak the language. And I think... well, one or two things he said, I think he saw me as a detective first and a black man second, you know?"

"Really?"

"Yeah. Like I was one of the good ones. Lucky for me, I guess."

"Huh."

"Yeah. Perils of the job, right?"

"How so?"

"Oh, c'mon. You ever notice another black man in the bull-pen?" Fuller asked with an annoyed toss of his head. "And not one giving a statement or being questioned. A black detective?"

Lennox had to admit that he hadn't.

"And… you ever notice you never noticed?"

Again, he had to say no.

"Yeah, well…" Fuller said. "Anyway, I gotta go."

"Where are you off to?" Lennox asked awkwardly.

"I got roped into judging a jack-o-lantern contest at the hotel this afternoon," Fuller shook his head sadly. "Winner gets to be in a parade next week. Gonna be a long day. Probably need something more than coffee to get through."

"Well, have fun."

"No chance. Good luck with Paiva."

"Thanks, Ed."

On his way out, Ed stopped to hold the door for someone coming in. Magnus Moon. Ed gave Lennox an apologetic smile as he went.

"Constable," Magnus said, hooking Lennox's arm with the crook of a serpent-headed cane. "Such a fortuitous synchronicity. Have you made any progress in your inquiry?"

"I can't really go into that, Mr. Moon. But we are following up on some very promising leads."

"*Reverend* Moon," Magnus smiled. "And let us once again assure you that no one in our community had a hand in this."

"I'll bear it in mind."

"And we don't know if this helps you at all," Magnus went on in a conspiratorial whisper. "But we believe he was a visitor. Not a local, but a visitor. A visitor, not a tourist, if you see what we mean."

"And what makes you say that?"

"We sense it. We sense it very strongly."

Magnus's royal we thing meant that Lennox could never be quite sure if he was only speaking for himself.

"I see."

"We wish him surrounded by white light as he begins his journey to the next world..."

"Me, too. Were you in town last weekend... Rev. Moon?"

"Of course. This time of year, we can never get away for so much as a moment. You know we run two Wiccan shops and are opening a third, and during the high season we seem to spend all of our time putting out fires, as it were. But busy as we are, we still managed to make our pilgrimage here."

"You come here a lot?"

"Daily. Especially on Sunday mornings—we make our way here, lured by the baked goods. The muffins and the scones are simply to die for, inspector."

"I—I'm sure they are."

Antonio Ramirez was a tall and angular Puerto Rican, twenty-five-ish, with thick dark hair and a thin goatee, folded up in a rickety chair in the parking garage booth. He shifted uncomfortably when Lennox came walking up to the booth and showed his gold detective's badge.

"I didn't do nothing," he said. He only seemed to be half-joking.

Lennox half-laughed and said he was looking into Annalisa's murder.

"Yeah, like I said, I didn't do nothing." This time he wasn't joking at all.

"Where were you that night, Antonio?"

"I said all this at the time. Me and Carlo were out that night. That other detective didn't believe me, but Carlo would back me up."

"Would?"

"He went back to San Juan a couple years ago. Family still has a house there. He didn't like it here. Too cold, rains all the time, too many stupid tourists."

"I know they brought you two in and questioned you, but neither of you were ever arrested."

"Damn straight. Doesn't mean they didn't still think I did it, that I… that I killed her." His voice caught slightly. "Doesn't mean *you* don't think that."

"Mrs. Paiva doesn't think you did."

"No," Antonio said quietly. "No. She's a good lady."

"You visit her every Sunday when you get off work here."

"Yeah, I do." His eyes showed how surprised he was that Lennox knew this. "You talk to her?"

"A couple days ago. She doesn't think you hurt Annalisa."

"I would never hurt her. Dude, I loved her."

"But Mrs. Paiva thought you two had broken up. Why would you break up with her if you loved her?"

As he asked the question, he felt a phantom knot in his lower back, a knot that had been there every morning he woke up on the couch in the museum's back office, and he knew sometimes one partner decided for both.

"Other way around, dude," Antonio corrected. "She broke up with me."

"Why?"

"I think she met someone else."

"Who?"

"Like I know. Somebody at the school, probably."

"Were you okay with her going to school?"

"Why wouldn't I be? She was going to be a nurse. Beats being a garage attendant, you know? She was going to make something of herself."

"I have to say, Antonio, it doesn't look good. She breaks up with you, you go out drinking on the night she gets killed, the only person who can alibi you is your brother?" He shook his head. "I can see why Curwen wanted to talk to you."

"Yeah, but like you said, talked to me but never arrested me. He couldn't place me at the scene—that's what he kept saying. He couldn't place me at the scene. Because I wasn't there."

He leaned back in the chair and folded his arms. He did his best to ignore the detective and reached over to twist the knobs on the radio and the space heater.

And Lennox decided that he believed him.

The call came over the scanner amid a sharp hiss of static. A family disturbance. Elizabeth Harker noted the address, just a few streets away, and responded that Unit 10 was on its way. She hit the lights and siren and stepped on the gas.

In the cruiser's passenger seat, Patrick Foley smiled nervously. Harker just shook her head. Foley had been partnered with her for the past few days and still seemed unable to relax around her. Maybe he was still just too green, too new on the job—some recruits never adjusted to the rigors and the monotony of police work. Every conversation with him was forced, awkward. Maybe he was still just stumbling around trying to find his feet… or maybe he was scared of her.

He wouldn't be the first. Some people never quite got past her notoriety, her minor celebrity status, and she found she often had to work twice as hard to earn a little acceptance, a little trust. But she bled blue like the rest of them, so Foley could damn well calm down.

She pulled up to the address given by the dispatcher.

The Musgrave mansion.

A nervous next-door neighbor squinted out from behind the curtains. Harker walked to the mansion's front door, big Maglite in one hand. She worked the lion's head knocker and stood back. Foley was a step behind her, one hand on his holstered weapon.

"*Police!*" Harker called.

"*Don't you open that door!*" a man's voice shouted from within.

But an instant later there was the grind of an ancient lock and the door was opened by a terrified woman gesturing the officers inside.

"Oh thank God," she breathed. "They're in here."

Harker and Foley pushed past her, and entered a room off the hallway, the only lighted room. The room the shouting came from.

"Now look what you've done you stupid, stupid boy," an old woman's voice snapped.

Harker quickly scanned the room. No weapons, no obvious threats. Just an old woman in a wheelchair and a tall middle-aged man, shaking and red in the face. The man glanced back and forth between the woman and the police. Harker's hand eased on the butt of the pistol on her hip.

"Is there a problem here?" she asked.

"I thought he was going to hit her," said the blonde woman who had opened the door. She stood behind the police, staying in the hallway outside the room. Still terrified.

"Okay. Names."

"I'm Agatha Musgrave, this is my stupid son Benedict and that little mouse over there is my daughter Laura. Now get the hell out of my house."

"And what were we arguing about tonight, ma'am?"

"Family business."

"And was your son here about to hit you over family business?"

"He wouldn't dare," Agatha said frostily.

"No, I would never hit Mother," Benedict said, barely above a whisper. He avoided Mother's gaze.

"You placed the call, ma'am?" Harker asked, turning to Laura.

Laura nodded, likewise unable to meet Agatha's gaze.

"You thought he was going to hit your mother?"

A stiff nod.

"And did he?"

A shake of the head. No.

"Ma'am, did he hit you?" Harker came back to Agatha.

"I already told you, he wouldn't dare."

"Do you wish to file a complaint at this time?"

"Of course not."

"Do you feel safe in this house without us?"

"Get out!"

Harker paused long enough to give each member of the family a hard look before nodding curtly.

"You have a good night now," she said.

"I'll log it in," Foley said when they got back to the cruiser.

"Please," Harker replied, looking back at the brick facade of the old house. Somehow, it seemed to be looking back at her. Eerie.

Chapter XI

FIRST THING MONDAY MORNING, Lennox made the short walk from the old jail to City Hall. The city was quiet, for now, and he enjoyed the cool breeze, the skittering of the dry leaves, and the faint smell of woodsmoke from somewhere. Despite the crass and crowded crush of the season in Salem, the noise and the crowds and the wreck they left behind them, he still loved autumn.

City Hall had stood on Washington Street since 1837, making it the second oldest city hall in the nation. Its smooth gray façade, crowned by a golden eagle, was stately, dignified; Greek Revival pilasters and stone wreaths along the roofline kept it from being simply a featureless gray block. Lennox made his way up the stairs and down the narrow central corridor to the city clerk's office, closing the leather-padded door behind him as he entered.

"I need to see a probate file and some vital records," he told the woman behind the counter.

The woman, every inch the bored municipal employee, didn't even look up from her magazine.

"Probate files are open—the index is over there. Vital records are confidential, not open to the public." She popped her gum expertly. "You a family member?"

Lennox reached into his pocket and tapped his gold badge on the countertop.

"I'm with the police, working a homicide investigation," he said evenly. "And I need those files."

She jumped up from her desk, partially startled but mostly just annoyed. She glanced at him and he hoped she didn't recognize him from the news. She didn't seem to. She probably didn't even pay attention to the news.

He wrote down Patience Musgrave's name and asked for her death certificate and any probate or guardianship files relating to her. He wasn't sure what the files might hold, but in any investigation it was always better to have too much information than too little.

The woman glanced at the name and wrinkled her nose.

"These are the same files that guy asked for last week," she said.

"What guy?" Lennox asked. He slid Paul Mather's photo out of his organizer. "This guy?"

"Yeah. He was here Friday. Like all day practically."

She turned to a stack of request forms at the far end of the counter. After a moment she handed over three.

The previous Friday afternoon, someone had requested copies of Patience Musgrave's death certificate, guardianship file, and the will of a Charles Musgrave. All three forms were signed Paul J. Mather. It gave Lennox a chill.

"I need to see these," he said.

"I think they're still over here," the woman said. "Yeah, they were in the wayback and it's wicked dusty back there so I was waiting for someone else to put them away."

"That's nice. If I could just see them, please?"

She handed them over and he spent the next two hours going through them, one onionskin page after another, manual typewriting faded with the years, making notes as he went.

According to the paperwork in the file, Patience Anne Musgrave had been declared mentally incompetent on April 8, 1967, at age sixteen, and committed to Danvers State Hospital the following day, one of hundreds of such patients consigned to the overcrowded, underfunded and short-staffed hospital. Her mother, Agatha Cabot Musgrave, was appointed her legal guardian. According to the file, Patience twice contested her status in the next few years, filing papers to reverse the decision and release her from the hospital. The court rejected her petitions, and she remained committed, under Agatha's legal guardianship.

Also in the file was a copy of Patience's death certificate, stating that she had died in the hospital infirmary, succumbing to ovarian cancer on March 22, 1982. She was forty-five years old. Lennox shook his head sadly; *he* was going to be forty-five next year. Patience was buried in the cemetery on the hospital grounds, in plot number one-thirty-seven.

He turned to the will of Charles Musgrave, which Mather had also requested. An older relative, clearly. Some of those old Yankee families recycled the same names and they leap-frogged down the generations. Mather's adoptive sister Danielle had said there was some possibility of an inheritance, and Lennox began to page through the will, searching. He found it fairly quickly, after skimming through the ritual sound-mind-and-body boilerplate and small bequests:

> *SECTION the FOURTH: The remainder of my estate, totaling $757,423.26, shall be held in trust for the benefit of Mr. George Linnell of Hyannis, Massachusetts, my roommate at Harvard, best man at my wedding, and good friend through good times and bad. In the event of George's death, the trust shall benefit my beloved niece Patience Anne Musgrave, upon reaching her 21st birthday. She should use this money as she wishes, but I recommend she devote a portion of it to distancing herself from her father, my useless brother Phillip, and his harridan wife, Agatha.*

Lennox laughed out loud. He couldn't quite believe the wording of that section had been allowed to stand, but he was glad that it did. Maybe the lawyer had met Phillip and Agatha and didn't like them, either. He started to like curmudgeonly old Uncle Charles.

Phillip Xavier Musgrave had been dead and in his grave for half a dozen years now, but Lennox still remembered seeing him being driven around town in a long back car with curtained windows. Phillip's lantern-jawed face had been twisted in a perpetual scowl and he always looked like he should be wearing a top hat, with a monocle screwed into one eye. Phillip was someone who showed up to city council meetings to angrily voice his opposition to any proposal, an embittered old man whose only answer was ever *No.* An embittered old man who sat in silent scorn as the rest of Salem crossed the street to avoid him.

Two death certificates were included in the folder with the will. The first showed that Uncle Charles Musgrave had died on November 28, 1965 of a massive heart attack. He was fifty-eight years old.

The second certificate was for George Linnell. He had died only a few days later, on December 2. He was fifty-seven.

A yellowed newspaper clipping fluttered out of the folder. Lennox picked it up from under the chair where it had landed and carefully unfolded it. It was brittle with age, and a corner snapped off. He read it over. Twice.

He slid the files back across the counter.

"I'm going to need copies of everything," he said.

Lieutenant Winters closed his office door and asked, "How's he doing, Michelle?"

Not only had he invited her to sit down in the leather armchair reserved for visitors, never subordinates, but he had also used her first name. This indicated the question was probably more personal than professional.

Ouellette considered her response for a moment.

"He seemed a little disoriented the first day back," she said. "Uncertain. But he found his feet pretty quickly. I think he's just glad to be back on the job."

"I gave him Paiva to work on, to get his feet wet again. Obviously, nobody was expecting this Gallows Hill case to come up."

"He's mentioned Paiva."

"Is he making progress?"

"He hasn't said much about it," she replied. "I'm sure it's on his mind."

"I did not want him going out on an active case, Michelle."

The continued use of her first name made it clear that this was not an official reprimand, more a registering of personal disapproval.

"He knows Paiva is just busywork. But we were the only ones in the bullpen when that call came in—everyone else was out on call or in court on that drug bust. I'm primary and I need his help. It's my call. You really can't underestimate him."

Lennox's high school English teacher look tricked people into underestimating him all the time. She had learned this herself years ago, on the first case where they'd been partnered together to investigate; Lennox had proven to be so much sharper than he appeared to be at first. He'd noticed that an upstairs clock disagreed with the downstairs clock by seven minutes, something that proved crucial to cracking a suspect's alibi.

"He might solve them both on the same day and walk in here like the conquering hero," she said. "You never know with him."

"Does he seem okay to you?"

"Was he okay before?" she asked. Anyone else would have asked the question with a smirk, but not Ouellette. "He's had a rough year, and he's always been... Lennox. He's been jittery, though. He keeps playing with that spike, keeps tapping it on his desk. That's... annoying."

Winters smiled, secretly pleased that someone was getting under Ouellette's near-imperturbable calm.

"But is he okay?"

"Don't know yet. He's taking on a lot. He definitely thinks he has something to prove. Right now he's in his find-out-everything mode. It's part of his... process. He doesn't usually tell me what he's thinking, not until he's ready."

"You're the ranking officer, he should be reporting to you every step of the way."

"Right. But it's not how we work together. And I don't need to remind you that he and I have the highest closure rate in the CID."

"Keep an eye on him, Michelle."

"I will. And…"

"And?"

"I don't think he's given us the full story on the shooting. There's something there he's not talking about."

Winters rubbed his chin.

"Such as?"

"I don't know. But he's holding something back."

"His report was filed and accepted, the AG did not regard it as a criminal shooting, and Morrow cleared him to return to duty. Are you saying we need to take another look at this?"

"No. I'm certainly not losing any sleep over a drug dealer who got shot during a raid. But there's something else there, and he's not telling me about it."

"If it becomes an issue, you will tell me. Until such time, there's nothing to talk about."

"Yes, sir."

"And here he comes now," Winters said, nodding to the window that looked out over the bullpen. Lennox was just coming in with a sheaf of photocopies tucked under one arm. "Thank you, Detective Sergeant Ouellette."

"You're welcome, sir."

"Scully made bail this morning and I assume went back home to Dorchester," Ouellette told Lennox as she returned to her desk out in the bullpen.

"Did you ask the Boston PD to keep an eye on him?"

"I asked, but it's… Dorchester."

"And they already have enough to do," he nodded. Dorchester had a reputation for being a rougher place than Salem could ever be.

"Right. And then there's this."

She handed over a copy of Harker's incident report on the domestic disturbance at the mansion the night before.

"It's been busy over there," he murmured.

"Right. The Lieutenant just signed off on placing a 48-hour surveillance on the family," she said. "With everything going on, I think we need to keep a very close watch on them. And maybe it'll give us something we can use. They'll recognize our faces, so I'm having Dworaczyk handle it. Surveillance teams will report to him, and he'll report to me." She gestured to the papers Lennox had come in with. "What do you have there?"

"I spent the morning over at city hall, and have I got a story for you," Lennox began. "Patience Musgrave entered Danvers State in April of 1967. She had been declared mentally incompetent, and placed under the legal guardianship of her mother, Agatha."

Ouellette pulled up their information on the victim.

"He's born on July 22, 1967," she said. "Patience is already pregnant when they have her committed. An unwed mother would shame the family back then—especially a family like that."

"It gets better. Her rich old uncle, Charles Musgrave, writes her into his will—Uncle Charles leaves his fortune to his college roommate. But if the roommate dies early, it all goes to his favorite niece, Patience. He hates her parents, which must be an interesting story in and of itself, and does not leave them a penny. It all goes to Patience."

"Such a nice family."

"So the roommate dies, and now Patience, the daughter who does not live up to the family name, is in line to inherit just over three quarters of a million dollars when she turns twenty-one. Her pregnancy gives the family an easy two-for-one solution."

"Sending her away and getting control over the three-quarters of a million that Patience stands to inherit in a few years' time."

"Patience has her baby," Lennox went on, "naming him Charles after her favorite uncle, and Agatha immediately puts the little bastard offspring, and potential heir to the family fortune, right up for adoption."

"Because Patience, poor dear, can't make legal decisions for herself," Ouellette nodded. "No indication of who the father is?"

"No. An out-of-wedlock birth will only be on record at the state level—I'll put in a request, but it'll take a while and whoever he is, he probably won't be listed on the birth certificate anyway.

"A couple of years later, Patience petitions the court to reverse its decision, cancel the guardianship, and let her leave the hospital. There's paperwork in the file that she found a doctor willing to sign off on this, but it was opposed by the doctor who originally declared her incompetent. Probably the old Musgrave family doctor. Court sides with the family, Patience remains under guardianship and stays locked up. Same thing happens again a couple of years later—she finds another doctor to vouch for her. The original doctor opposes it and the court turns her down. Patience is obviously far from incompetent, she was just an obstacle between them and the money."

"What eventually happened to her?"

"Dies in 1982, cancer. She's buried in the hospital cemetery, not in the family plot. And now all these years later, Patience's long lost son shows up. Maybe asking where his share of the money is, or maybe just wanting to know what the hell they did to his mother. Maybe he threatens to expose the whole story."

"And the family panics."

"People do stupid things to hang onto three-quarters of a million dollars," Lennox shrugged. "Or to keep family secrets buried."

"So what happened to the college friend?"

Lennox pulled the photocopy of the newspaper clipping out of the pile of papers on her desk. Ouellette read it over and bit her lip.

"*Merde.*"

Four days after Uncle Charles Musgrave's death from a heart attack, George Linnell was killed on an icy Boston street by a hit-and-run driver.

Chapter XII

LENNOX KNEW THAT TWO DAYS was probably not long enough to get anything useful, but he also knew they couldn't afford to wait much longer than that. More of the usual hurry-up-and-wait that took up so much of a cop's time. Still, he could at least try to put the time to good use.

"Plunkett," he called across the bullpen. "Where would I find Curwen, if I needed to?"

Detective Sergeant Plunkett was nearing retirement age, and served as the department's institutional memory. He went out on as few calls as possible.

"He likes to fish off the pier out at the Willows," he said.

The Willows was a park jutting out into the waters of Salem Sound.

"Seriously? It's almost November."

"You asked," Plunkett shrugged. "You going to ask him about the Paiva thing?"

"Yeah."

"Good luck with that."

"How do you mean?"

"Pointless going over it. Boyfriend did it."

"And yet the case is still open, six years later."

Plunkett muttered dismissively as Lennox left the bullpen.

The Willows had been named for the trees planted on the grounds of the smallpox hospital which eventually became the park over a century ago. Today, where patients once convalesced, kids played, boardwalk restaurants advertised cheap eats, and pathways wound lazily along the beaches. Back when they first settled in Salem, Lennox and Ellen would bring Allison here on the weekends. They went swimming or walking or to a concert; he remembered going to half a dozen concerts with them, at the angular zig-zag bandshell. He couldn't remember the bands or the music now. All he could remember was that he had been here with his wife and their daughter, and they had laughed and held hands and felt the warm summer sun on their skin. Together.

The boardwalk shops usually closed after Labor Day, but a few of them stayed open to catch the tourist trade on October weekends. The greasy scent of a chop suey sandwich reminded him that he hadn't had breakfast. The rows of benches at the bandshell were as empty as the parking lot when he arrived. He made his way down a path that led to the pier looking out over the Sound. In the summer, tourists would have posed for pictures and a dozen boats would have been moored at the base of the pier, bobbing up and down on the tide. But on a graying October day, there were no tourists, no boats, only a few old men with fishing rods scattered here and there along the length of the pier. A couple of them chatted in Portuguese, another pair in Spanish, and Lennox passed them by, making his way toward the solitary figure in one corner. Ed Curwen.

Curwen was bundled up against the misty air in a long oiled rain slicker and tweed cap. He stared off down the length of the fishing rod, seeming not to care if the fish were biting or not. Fishing was a religion to some, Lennox knew; back in the Coast Guard, he'd spent enough nights in high January seas pulling fishing boats off rocky shoals and shallows. Next to him, in a basket, were several long neck beer bottles. The pear-shaped Curwen had spent thirty-two years on the force, the majority of it as a detective. He retired a year after Lennox came into the CID, and they only knew one another slightly.

"Andrew Lennox, as I live and breathe," Curwen said, smiling unhappily. "Taking up fishing on your time off?"

"No, I'm back, actually."

"That was quick."

"It was three weeks."

Curwen scowled. "Hard to keep track of time when you're retired," he said.

"Plunkett told me I could find you out here."

"I'm usually out here," Curwen said, quietly adding, "Not after dark, though."

The Willows was the most notorious cruising site in the city after sunset, and when he was still back in uniform Lennox had answered a number of calls reporting lewd behavior in the twilit park.

"So... what the hell happened with you anyway?"

"Don't really want to talk about it," Lennox replied.

"Fair enough. One more dead drug dealer, who the fuck cares. How's Ouellette? She still got that ass on her?"

Lennox didn't answer. Apparently, Dworaczyk wasn't the only one checking out his partner.

"Now that I'm back, the old man gave me a cold case to work."

Curwen rolled his eyes. "Till you prove you're ready to go back to work for real."

"Yeah, something like that, I guess."

"What case?"

"Paiva."

Curwen set his pole down and leaned heavily against the railing. He took a long pull from the beer bottle at his elbow, emptying it. He threw the bottle out into the water, half-aiming for a Canada goose paddling by. He took two bottles out of the basket, keeping one for himself and handing the other to Lennox.

"They think I missed something?" he asked, looking out over the choppy water.

"Nothing like that," Lennox said. "Just a second pair of eyes." But Lennox knew that a second pair of eyes rarely saw anything other than what the first pair already had. "Guy's still out there somewhere, obviously."

"Yeah, in the booth at the parking garage," Curwen snapped, rubbing his unshaven chin.

"So you still think it was him?"

"Yeah, but we couldn't place him at the scene. And he had that half-assed alibi from his brother, who fucked off back to the Dominican."

"Puerto Rico," Lennox said quietly.

"Yeah, whatever. Never believed him anyway. You drinking that or not?"

Lennox regarded the bottle uncertainly. The phrase *Alcohol May Intensify Effects*, from the warnings on the Xanax box, came to mind. The thought made him queasy. He set the unopened bottle down on the railing.

"I'm on duty," he said. "So, did you question anyone else?"

"Didn't need to. It was him."

"Motive?"

"She was going to school, getting away from fucking Ward Street, leaving the neighborhood boys behind. She didn't need him, he couldn't handle it. That crime scene had crime-of-passion written all over it. You saw the photos—they're in the file."

"Yeah, I saw them. You're right. Crime-of-passion. Absolutely."

Silence.

"Was there anything you left out of the reports?" Lennox asked uncomfortably, staring at the brown bottle balanced on the weathered railing.

The ultimate cop rule—if it wasn't in the report, it didn't happen.

"Things always get left out," Curwen replied quietly. "You leave anything out of your final report on that shooting?"

Lennox took a deep breath and asked, "Okay, so what got left out?"

"He says she broke up with him."

"Yeah, that's in there."

"Word was that she got involved with one of the professors over at the school," Curwen said. "Got this from a couple of her friends."

"And you followed up on that?"

"Of course we did. Peter Prescott. Teaches in the history department, or at least he did then."

Of course he taught in the history department. So did Ellen. So did the man Ellen left him for.

"We talked to him," Curwen went on. "But he was at some concert the night she got killed. Everybody saw him. Waste of time talking to him. His alibi was better than the kid's. I'm telling you, the kid did it. Little fucking spick."

Silence again.

"So you find anything new yet?"

"Not yet. But I'll… I'll keep you informed."

"Yeah."

Lennox walked away, leaving the unopened bottle there on the railing. They both knew he was lying.

The Avalon Danvers, the apartment complex that had once been the psychiatric hospital where Patience Musgrave gave birth to her son and lived out the remainder of her short, sad life, stood atop Hathorne Hill, looking regally out over the town of Danvers spread below.

Danvers State Hospital opened in 1874, in the next town over from Salem, in what had once been Salem Village, home of the afflicted girls and accused witches three centuries earlier. It was a hulking brick edifice of gables, towers, and long tall windows, beautiful in an elaborate and grimly Dickensian way. Almost from the beginning, the facility had been overcrowded and understaffed. It became a warehouse for unfortunates and castoffs—retarded children and adults, elderly Alzheimer's sufferers, neurotics, schizo-phrenics, manic-depressives, and others who were just beyond their family's ability to care for, or to cope with. As the population grew and budget cuts slashed the staff, dark rumors began to circulate about abuse and neglect; it was said to be the birthplace of the frontal lobotomy, and there were of course B-movie whispers of straitjackets and electroshock and padded cells, of abusive orderlies and patients who simply vanished on a dark and stormy night. The stories that swirled about the place were probably no more accurate than the legends that surrounded the witch trials.

The hospital had closed over twenty years ago, and soon became a favorite destination for partying teenagers and self-styled paranormal investigators running around in the dark and claiming to have encountered ghosts. Supposedly, former patients returned to camp out on the grounds, claiming that the hospital was the only home they'd ever known.

Lennox parked in one of the long shadows cast by the main building, locked his doors, and hoped that wasn't true. But some rumors always were. Even ones about cops.

Patience herself would have recognized very little of the place now. Many of the buildings she knew had been torn down by the developers and replaced with faceless white apartment blocks. But the massive Kirkbride building, the looming centerpiece of both the old hospital and the new development, still stood tall and proud. The brick tower frowned down on him as Lennox turned his back on it and began to pick his way down a muddy path leading into the woods at the edge of the property.

Naked tree branches shivered against a gray woolen sky as he reached the bottom of the path. He paused by a boulder, one side flat, polished smooth and chiseled with the words, *The Danvers State Hospital Cemetery: The Echos They Left Behind.*

He wondered briefly how much they had paid the engraver who misspelled *echoes.*

Beyond the boulder lay an open field, a few hundred yards on a side, bounded by a low field-stone wall. Looking out over the gently sloping ground, carpeted in bright dry leaves, gave him a chill. Graveyards always did. They always gave him the troubling feeling that he was both completely alone, and anything but alone.

The original wooden grave markers were long gone, from what he had read, and now no one could be entirely certain which body was buried where. In the middle of the field, near some bare trees, stood three granite blocks and a bench. Coming closer, he could see the mounted bronze plaques listing name after name after name—the dead, buried somewhere here. There were over two hundred names listed on the headstone-like blocks; he wondered how many more were still unlisted. Patience was easy to find, alphabetical order placing her in the middle of the list.

He swept leaves from a small bronze rectangle set into the ground at his feet. Number fifteen. Turning around and taking a step away, he uncovered number seventy-five. He stood up, scanning the field and calculating rows in his head, counting as he walked.

He saw the flowers as he approached the spot, a crumbling bouquet of lilies tied with a faded blue ribbon, stark and pale against the fallen leaves. The flowers lay diagonally across the plaque marked one-thirty-seven..

Patience's grave.

He straightened up and took a deep breath as the blood rushed back into his head.

Charles, the long-lost Musgrave, visiting his mother's grave, bringing her flowers. Flowers for the mother he had never known.

Lennox heard a thump behind him and whirled, his hand diving reflexively into his coat, where his S&W .40 caliber service weapon hung from his belt.

Someone had climbed over the low stone wall at the edge of the field, landing clumsily. A middle-aged man in an oversize sweatshirt, with a curiously blank expression on his round face, his mouth half-open. Blunt features like an unfinished portrait. He crossed the field to where Lennox stood, moving with a strange halting gait, like a giant toddler.

"Hi," he said, too loudly. "My name's Daniel. Danny for short. What's yours?"

Lennox took a deep breath. The man was retarded. Apparently, some of the former patients really did come back.

"Andrew…" he replied, adding, "Andy for short."

"Hi, Andy."

"Hi, Danny," he said lamely. "Did you use to live here?"

"Yup. I came here to live on February 9, 1971. It was a Tuesday. I was nine. I was born on May 14, 1962. That was a Thursday. I was here till they closed the hospital. I left on June 30, 1992. Another Tuesday. I lived here for seven thousand six hundred and seventy days. That's a long time, right?"

"It is."

Danny looked around nervously, out of things to say. He looked down to the plaque at Lennox's feet.

"One thirty seven," he said. "That's Patience. Patience Anne Musgrave. She came here on April 9, 1967. It was Thursday. She didn't remember, but it was Thursday. I told her. She was already here when I came. She had a baby. July 8, 1967. Wednesday. That was before I came to live here. She was my friend. She was nice."

"You knew her?"

"She was my friend," Danny repeated. "She was nice. She used to give me her red jello."

Lennox smiled. "She didn't like red jello?"

"No, she liked it. But I like it more. She knew. She used to give me hers."

"You liked her, didn't you, Danny?" Lennox smiled.

"No," he replied, too quickly. "Not like-like. Just like."

"It's okay, I won't tell anyone. Did anybody ever come visit her here at the hospital, Danny?"

If anyone ever had, no doubt Danny would know who it was and exactly when they had been here.

"No." Danny was shifting his weight from one foot to the other, back and forth. "She got sick," he added sadly, quietly, staring at the ground. "She died March 22, 1982. Monday." He pointed to the next plaque over. "Number one thirty six, that's George Stewart, died Saturday, September 17, 1983. He was here for eight thousand forty-five days. Longer than me. Number one thirty eight, that's Mary Lacey. She died August 9, 1984. It was

Thursday. She was here only one hundred forty-four days. She wasn't nice," he wrinkled his nose.

Awkward silence.

"So what are you doing here, Danny?"

"I like it here," he replied. "I'm here all the time. Last time was yesterday. Why are you here?"

"I came to visit Patience."

"Did you know her?"

"No, but I'm kind of her friend right now. Wait—you're here all the time? Did you see who... gave her these flowers, Danny?"

"Saturday, the 17th. He was here. He was wearing a leather jacket. Him and the lady gave Patience the flowers and stood there for a little while. They looked sad."

"The lady?"

"The blonde lady," Danny said cautiously. "The blonde lady with him. They didn't see me. But I saw them."

The blonde lady. Laura. Danny could put Laura with the victim.

"Danny—would you know the blonde lady if you saw her again?"

"Maybe..."

Dammit. The photos were back at the station; he didn't think to bring them along. He didn't know he was going to stumble across a potential witness in a graveyard.

"Danny, I'm a policeman." He took out his badge and held it up. "See? Can you come back to my police station with me and look at a picture? It's really important."

"You don't have a uniform," Danny said.

"I'm not that kind of policeman. I really need your help, Danny..."

"I... I have to go," Danny stammered. He turned to run heavily across the graveyard and clamber over the stone wall.

Lennox took a few steps after him and then stopped. He had no jurisdiction in Danvers, no authority here. He couldn't take Danny into custody and bring him back to the station. And he wasn't about to go chasing a retarded guy through the woods, begging him to come with him.

He trudged back up the path, past the misspelled boulder, weak in the knees. He fished a blister-pack out of his jacket pocket and put a Xanax under his tongue. He sat in the car for a good fifteen minutes, head against the steering wheel, before he felt able to drive.

Chapter XIII

HE CALLED THE DANVERS POLICE when he got back to the station, asking to speak with the lieutenant in the patrol division.

"I need you to keep an eye out for someone," he said. "A mentally retarded guy named Danny. You know him?"

"Danny Dateline," Lieutenant Michaelson said. "Everybody knows him. What do you need him for?"

"You probably heard about the body out at Gallows Hill? Danny can place someone with the victim, we just need him to make an ID."

"He'll give you the exact date and time, too," Michaelson said. "Where did you see him?"

"Over at the old Danvers State. In… in the graveyard."

"He's outside a lot this time of year."

"But you know where he lives?"

"Not exactly. He kind of comes and goes. There are a few places we know he likes to hang out, so we'll check there for you. Shouldn't be a problem. He's a good kid."

"He's older than I am," Lennox said.

"Right."

"Good news and bad news," he said to Ouellette, hanging up the phone. "I found someone who can put Laura and the victim together. The bad news is… he's retarded."

"Not exactly a reliable witness," she said.

"You wouldn't think that if you met him. He actually seems really sharp. Yes, a lawyer will tear him apart, but right now he's the best we can do. If we can find him; he lives over in Danvers. They're looking for him."

"If he saw them together, that only puts suspicion on her, not the rest of the family."

"Thin end of the wedge," Lennox replied, turning to an envelope that had come in while he was on the phone. A padded manila mailer with too many stamps, addressed to him in blocky, anonymous handwriting—*Det. Andrew Lennox, Salem Police Department, 95 Margin Street, Salem MA, 01970.*

No return address. Of course. Pressing it carefully, he felt something stiff inside, narrow, three or four inches long.

He tugged a pair of blue latex gloves from the box on his desk and snapped them on. Using the marlinspike, he slowly tore open the end away from the flap, and shook the contents out onto his desk.

An index card and a key.

"You order the weirdest stuff on Amazon," Ouellette murmured.

"Not this time…"

The card read, *"Charles Musgrave was murdered in the family home on Sunday Oct. 18. The proof you need is in the family Bible."*

It was in the same handwriting as the address on the envelope, the same clunky block capitals everyone seemed to use when trying to disguise their handwriting.

The key was a car key, a late-model Toyota.

"What make was the rental car they found over in Beverly?"

"A Toyota Prius," Ouellette said without even checking her notes.

"Thought so."

He bagged the key and walked it down the hall to the fingerprint lab. Johnson was there, having coffee with their tech, a skinny man with tiny glasses and tattoos scrolling up his arms. They were laughing at some joke as he came into the room, hanging out, sharing the kind of easygoing camaraderie that Lennox realized, more and more, he lacked with anyone in the department.

"I need this dusted for prints. Right now. I'll wait."

"Okay."

The tech labored over the key for a few minutes, dusting and brushing and squinting, peering at it under lights and lenses.

"So," Johnson said quietly, taking a step away as the man worked, "how's it feel to be back?"

"Feels fine," he replied, not sure what else he could say.

"You've had kind of a rough year. I mean, your divorce went through a little while ago, right?"

"Not quite a year."

"So... it's all behind you."

"Um, sure. I guess."

It was anything but.

"Can ask you a personal question?"

"Sure, Johnson."

"You... seeing anyone?"

Lennox let out a slow breath. So that's where this was going. "I'm... not."

"There's an opening reception at the Peabody-Essex for the new exhibit—the surrealists," she said. Nervousness showed in the speed of her speech. "Don't know if you saw it in the news."

"Kind of avoiding the news lately."

"Well, anyway, I have an extra ticket." She gave a small smile. "I don't know if you're into art, or the surrealism, but it looks like a good show and we could maybe grab a bite down at Rockafella's after?"

Johnson was pretty, with shaggy blonde bangs and freckles across the bridge of her nose. A nose not at all like Ellen's. Pixieish, one of those women who still looked like a college girl even as she left age forty somewhere behind her.

"Um, well, you see..." he laughed uncomfortably. "I'm right in the middle of this case, you know, and can't really... um..."

"Gotcha," she said unhappily, turning back to the tech. "Anything?"

"Nah. Wiped clean."

"Thanks," Lennox said, taking it back.

"Let me know if you change your mind," she called after him as he headed down the corridor, back to the bullpen.

"Take a ride?" he asked Ouellette.

"Where are we going?"

"You'll see," he said with a smile.

Twenty minutes later, they stood together in the back lot the Beverly Police Department used for an impound yard. A tired and slightly puzzled uniformed officer pointed out the blue Prius, wondering what two Salem detectives wanted with it.

The Prius sat between a rusted out hulk and a wrecked Ford; the spiderweb shatter sprawled across the windshield made Lennox's stomach flutter. Lennox tried to ignore it and fitted the key into the Prius's lock. The door opened.

"Thought so," he said. "Whoever wrote that note was the person who dumped this car. And they witnessed the murder."

"A witness who does not want to be a witness," Ouellette nodded.

Lennox started up the car and checked the last address in the dashboard GPS. The Hawthorne. As Dworaczyk had reported after he and Johnson had checked out the car last week.

"So he's killed in the house, and the body is left at Gallows Hill and the car left here. It'd be nice if the Musgrave address was in the GPS," Ouellette said. "That'd help place him at the scene."

Lennox sat in the driver's seat for a long moment, eyes closed.

"Salem is a good walking town, especially this time of year with the leaves and the decorations. I like walking around downtown this time of year, even with the crowds," he said. "So let's assume he finds out where the Musgrave mansion is and walks there Saturday. He wakes up Sunday morning and it's raining, so he takes the car. He already knows where the family home is so he doesn't need the GPS which is why the address isn't in there."

"That makes sense," Ouellette nodded.

"And... didn't these two things always seem to not quite match?"

"What do you mean?"

"We have a body elaborately staged out at Gallows Hill. Not just anywhere, but Gallows Hill. Hanging, with pentagrams on the palms. That's someone with... shall we say a morbid imagination? And then we have a car left in a parking lot in Beverly. Much more... prosaic? Two very different people."

"You think Benedict left the body and Laura was in charge of the car?"

"I do indeed."

"Again, it makes sense. But why go back Sunday?"

"They lured him back. They gave him a reason to come back. He trusted them."

"The last mistake he ever made," Ouellette said quietly.

On Wednesday, Dworaczyk gave his first surveillance report.

"This is a very exciting assignment for the guys, I can tell you," he said. "They are very happy to have been picked."

"What did you find?" Ouellette asked.

"The whole time, the old lady never leaves the house. Not once. The son comes out to get the mail, and to sign for a grocery delivery."

"They have the groceries delivered?" Lennox asked with a smirk.

"Hey, can you honestly picture any of those people in the supermarket?"

"Fair point."

"Yesterday afternoon, son comes out, slams the door, and stands on the front step all pissed-off looking. Then he shoves his hands in his pockets and stomps off downtown, to Essex Street."

Essex Street was a main street downtown, one of the original streets laid out centuries before. Several blocks were closed to traffic, forming a pedestrian mall near the Hawthorne Hotel and the

Peabody Essex Museum, lined with tourist shops and restaurants. It was a busy enough street any day of the year, but in October it was thick with tourists and day-trippers.

"One of the guys in plainclothes follows him. Son goes into one of the tourist shops." Dworaczyk checked his report. "Pendragon's."

"You're kidding?"

"No, I am not. He goes in, our guy walks by and doubles back. Son is sitting in the front window… getting his tarot cards read."

Lennox laughed.

"Then what?" Ouellette asked.

"Then he heads back home, stopping to grab a sandwich on the way. And that is it. You have a fifty-something guy who lives with his mom in a creepy-ass old house that he leaves once, to get his tarot cards read," Dworaczyk concluded. "And that, I tell you, is not healthy."

"What about the sister?"

"We had Foley on her most of the time," Dworaczyk said, turning a page in the report. "Sister lives over in those posh new condos. They have enough parking spaces so it was easy for Foley to blend in. Each morning, coffee and a bagel at a place on Washington between nine and ten. Spends an hour or two at the family mansion every day. Walks the dog on the Common every afternoon at one o'clock, like clockwork. She does her own grocery shopping over at Whole Foods in Swampscott. Went to a 4H meeting on Wednesday afternoon. Husband works downtown. Leaves every morning at 8:30 a.m., home between 4:30 and 5:00 p.m. I kept an eye on him yesterday. I would bet you a dollar he is sleeping with his secretary."

"Anything else?" Ouellette asked.

"No. That is it. Not much you can use in all of this."

"More than you'd think," Lennox said.

Dworaczyk stood to go, sneaking an up-and-down glance at Ouellette as he did so. Elevator eyes.

"We should head over to Pendragon's and see what we can see over there," Ouellette said as Dworaczyk handed in his report, straightened his tie, and returned to his desk.

"Can that wait until this afternoon?" Lennox asked, glancing at the clock. 11:47 a.m.

"You have something to do?"

"Going for a jog," he replied.

Chapter XIV

LENNOX TRIED TO HIT THE STATION'S GYM three or four times a week. Time on a treadmill or with weights gave his mind room to wander, and something about the repetition of simple physical activity was remarkably freeing. When he had been out on leave, he'd avoided the station entirely and had instead taken up jogging around Salem Common, doing laps in the early morning mist.

The Common consisted of some nine acres of open parkland dating to the early settlers. Bounded by an ornate wrought iron fence, there was a playground at one end and domed marble bandstand toward the other, with elegant lamp posts and a simple war monument and broad grassy sweeps. It was surrounded by landmarks—the Hawthorne, stately Samuel McIntire homes, an imposing bronze statue of Roger Conant, the city's Puritan founder. It had once been a cattle pasture, and later served as the militia's training ground. After the fire in 1914, thousands of residents who had lost everything camped out on the Common in an improvised tent city. They lived there for weeks, and some of them for months, tattered makeshift tents fluttering in the breeze.

The broad sidewalks at the main entrance made a little half-moon plaza, scattered with bright leaves, and now aluminum benches and portable toilets had been set up for the Halloween crowds. One small trailer, festooned with wheat sheaves and plastic jack-o-lanterns, was marked *Information*, with brochures and schedules held down on the countertop with rocks and bricks, and more taped and affixed to the sheet metal walls. *If only it were that easy,* Lennox thought—*getting what you needed to know by asking at a booth.* Similar trailers nearby sold cotton candy and fried dough. October in Salem was always a carnival—and earlier in the week, an actual carnival had set up in the riverfront park, raising a Ferris wheel and garish tents.

He pulled into a yellow *No Parking* zone at 12:50 and gulped down the last half of a bottle of water. He scanned the Common—three people walking dogs, none of them Laura. He stretched, pulled on a dark blue Salem PD sweatshirt, and set out on his run.

It was a chilly day, and the icy air made his lungs ache as he jogged along the iron fence. He'd spent most of his early-morning runs trying to catch his breath and hacking up nasty phlegm as his body slowly began to clean up from years of smoking. Today's run was somehow easier.

He spotted Laura and her golden retriever on his second lap. He slowed his pace so their paths would cross. The dog barked at him as he drew close and he hesitated.

Laura glanced apologetically at him before realizing who he was.

"Detective?" she asked.

"Yes? Oh, you're Laura Musgrave…"

"Gagnon," she corrected.

"Right, Gagnon. Sorry. That's a beautiful dog. What's his name?"

"Boba," she said, wrinkling her nose. "Boba Fetch. My husband named him, He thought it was funny. And he doesn't fetch anyway."

"My family had a golden when I was growing up. Great dogs," he said. It was a lie. His parents weren't dog people either.

"Did you grow up here?"

"No. I kind of grew up everywhere. Army brat."

"I see."

"My parents were both officers. Retired now," he said, trying to catch his breath. "There's been a Lennox in every war, according to family legend. I was kind of the black sheep—I was Coast

Guard. Chief Petty Officer Lennox, reporting for duty," he smiled and saluted. "The folks were disappointed I was doing something where I probably wasn't going to get shot at. But my brother's a lieutenant stationed in Kandahar right now, so there's that."

"You still must have some stories to tell."

"I was a coxswain, so I piloted vessels. We did safety inspections and rescues. I moved around, so I was on an icebreaker for a while, I went down to Florida and did drug interdictions, so there was some chance of getting shot at. At least the folks were happy."

"How long have you been with the police?"

"Nine years. Which is about twenty-two in cop years," he laughed. "You've been here all your life, obviously."

"Except four years at Barnard," she replied. "I wanted to get away for a while. Growing up in Salem with the Musgrave name… wasn't always easy. So I wanted to go somewhere I could just be me, not be that Musgrave girl. But the name did come in handy when applying."

He coughed and took a deep breath, coughing again.

"All this running makes me want a cigarette," he laughed, rubbing his chest.

"Would you like one?" she asked, taking a slim box of Dunhills from a coat pocket.

"Do you mind?"

"No…" she said awkwardly.

He lit the cigarette and handed the boxy gold lighter back to her. He inhaled deeply, and the smoke, crisp and dry like good champagne, worked its way down into him, caressing his lungs and his mind. Amazing. Delicious.

He realized then how much he had missed the solidarity that existed between smokers; you could always bum a cigarette off a fellow traveler, always click with a stranger over a smoke.

"These are nice," he nodded.

"Aren't they?" She lit one with hands that trembled.

Time to lower the boom.

"Laura, what were you and your nephew doing out at the old Danvers State graveyard last Saturday? The day before he was killed?"

"I don't know what you mean," she said too quickly. "I never saw him—"

"You were there with him. Someone saw you."

"No, I wasn't—"

"Yes, you *were*."

Silence.

"Laura, I don't think you had anything to do with this. I don't *think* you did. But—"

Boba barked and pulled on his leash.

"I should really get him home," she stumbled over her words.

"Laura…"

She walked away across the Common.

Lennox threw the smoldering Dunhill away like something that had bitten him.

Pendragon's was one of countless witch-kitsch shops expectantly lining Essex Street downtown, in the epicenter of the tourist trade. Halloween loomed a few days away, and tourists had been descending on the city like marines hitting Normandy. Some people booked a year in advance, saved all year, maxed out their credit cards, and traveled halfway around the world to spend Halloween in Salem. In addition to various occult shops, haunted houses, and walking tours headquartered along Essex, street vendors set up tents and carts to hawk t-shirts, face painting, and fried food.

Pendragon's was old enough to be an institution; the shop had opened its doors sometime in the seventies, one of the first businesses in town to cater to the nascent tourist industry, and it had waited patiently while the rest of downtown came around to its way of seeing things. It occupied a narrow gambrel roofed building, painted black, with long windows that watched crowds come and go below. The sign—with an Eye of Horus in one corner and either a crow or a raven in the other, Lennox couldn't tell which—promised *"Psychic Readings Within!"* The paint was beginning to chip. The line of querants eager to have their cards read snaked down the block.

"You've been smoking," Ouellette said as they approached the front of the line.

"Don't want to talk about it. Shall we go in?"

They were stopped at the front door by a perky young woman in a plunging leather corset, velvet Renaissance faire coat, and a tall conical hat trimmed in ostrich feathers; garments that were probably deep in a closet eleven months of the year. She smiled sweetly and tucked a strand of multicolored hair behind one ear. She wore skull-and-crossbone earrings, set with diamonds. If she showed any more cleavage, she'd need some kind of a permit.

"I'm sorry, my loves," she cooed. "But we have a line—"

"And we have these," Ouellette said, flashing her badge, cupped in one hand. "We need to talk to your boss. Now."

The young woman very carefully leaned around the edge of the black door and called, "Luna!", adding in a stage whisper, "*Police!*"

Luna, swathed in black and purple and with a Dunkin' Donuts coffee in one heavily beringed hand, appeared and ushered the detectives inside.

Lennox was immediately hit with the syrupy scent of patchouli and the drowsy notes of new age harp in the crowded little shop. Tourists packed the place, cash and credit cards in hand, and the cash register kept ringing and ringing and ringing. The shop's inventory was pretty much the same as at a dozen or more shops throughout downtown, but Pendragon's had long since become some kind of superstore. There were mojo bags, crystal shards, wands and books and bottles of essential oils arranged neatly on shelves and in display cases. Bundles of dried herbs hung from the roofbeams, priced as marked, and electric candles flickered from Gothic wall sconces.

He noticed a black t-shirt on the clearance rack. Under the words *Never Again!* in Old English script were listed all twenty victims of the witch trials, name following upon name. Lennox bit his lip. He wasn't sure the best way to remember those poor souls was to put them on a made-in-Thailand t-shirt, marked down to $16.92.

Luna motioned them into a back office. The fluorescent lights were a harsh contrast to the mood lighting out on the sales floor. Crystal balls and athames were carelessly scattered about amid toner cartridges and K-Cups for the coffee maker.

"What can I do for you officers?" she asked.

"Detectives," Ouellette said. "We understand that this man came in for a reading yesterday about eleven o'clock?"

She pulled Benedict Musgrave's DMV photo up on her smartphone, placing it on the cluttered break table in the middle of the room.

"All of our psychics are licensed," Luna said defensively.

Salem had begun issuing fortunetelling licenses in the 1930s, in theory to regulate the industry; Lennox always suspected it was simply a creative way to generate more revenue for a city still reeling from the Depression. Applying for a license entailed filling out a form, paying a fee, and passing a criminal background check. Proof of genuine psychic ability, or even of sincere belief in one's psychic ability, was not necessary. The license bearing the holder's name, photo, and information, was required by law to be prominently displayed; most wore it on their belts, or around their necks, like convention attendees.

Originally, there had been a cap on the number of psychics allowed to practice. Just a few years before, when the city council proposed to remove the cap, the move had been met with colorful resistance. Too many psychics would simply be pandering to the tourist trade, current license-holders said with a straight face, while those advocating removal of the cap insisted they had as much right as any to practice their ancient and deeply religious art form. It didn't take a detective to see that this was merely a question of economics and competition, and Lennox smiled as he recalled breaking up a fistfight on Essex Street between two psychics on opposite sides of the question.

"That's not what this is about," Ouellette said. "This man is a person of interest in an investigation, and we really need to speak with whoever he came to see. Now."

"I'll have to check the log," Luna said reluctantly.

Ouellette nodded and Luna left the room to come back a moment later with a worn leather ledger-book. She sipped from her coffee as she turned pages.

"How many of those have you had today?" Lennox asked, smiling and gesturing at the big styro cup.

"My favorite witches' brew," Luna muttered wearily. "It looks like he saw Symboline when he was here. Customers get to choose their reader. Yesterday was slow so we had her in the front window. Good advertising."

"Is she here today?"

"She is, but… okay, look, I need to point out that our readers are all independent contractors, and if she's engaged in anything illegal I don't know anything about it and my shop is not involved in any way."

"Duly noted. Where is she?"

"Come with me."

Luna steered the detectives through the shop to a room at the back. Behind a beaded curtain, half a dozen women sat at little draped tables, some with crystal balls, others with tarot cards or magnifying glasses and palmistry charts, one even with a laptop. But all had small tip jars. The readers were variously braided, bleached or dyed, with broomstick skirts and boots or caftans and sandals, and a small fortune spent in mascara. Several were in the middle of readings with clients—clients who ranged from cackling party girls out for a good time to misty-eyed seekers with serious queries.

This was a bizarre scene, Lennox thought. With the corseted greeter outside, the dim lighting, the incense and the soft music, the roomful of costumed women, pick the girl you like... it was like some kind of unearthly bordello.

"Symboline," Luna said to one of the few readers with no client. "These detectives would like to speak to you."

"Do they have an appointment?"

"They don't need one," Luna replied curtly. Clearly not happy. "You can talk out back."

Symboline led the detectives out a side door marked *No Exit! Alarm Will Sound* and into a brick alleyway behind the shop. No alarm sounded as the door closed behind them.

Her fortuneteller's license gave her name as Symboline Carto, but Lennox recognized her immediately as Donna Goldman. He had handled her background check when she arrived from Boulder four years ago and applied. She didn't seem to recognize him.

"We have some questions about this man." Ouellette showed her the photo of Benedict Musgrave. "We understand you read his cards yesterday?"

"Yes," she said. "He's come to me several times."

"This man is a person of interest in an investigation we're conducting, and we need to know what, if anything, he may have told you."

Symboline leaned back against the building's black clapboard wall and smiled.

"I'm sorry detective, but that's privileged."

"Really?" Lennox asked. "You're really going to go that route?"

Ouellette rolled her eyes. She knew this would happen. She'd told Lennox so in the car on the way over. And he'd agreed she was probably right.

"I was acting as his spiritual counselor," Symboline insisted.

"At forty dollars for a half hour," Lennox shook his head.

"Can't put a price on enlightenment, detective."

"Spiritual counselor? Seriously?"

"Seriously. Our communication is privileged, just as much as one between a priest or rabbi and a member of their congregation.

Speaking of which…" She reached into a pocket in her long skirt and came out with a small laminated card. A square of parchment, with an embossed seal and a pair of signatures, certifying that Symboline Carto was a full minister in good standing with the first Circle of Hecate, Salem, Massachusetts, with all the rights, privileges, and immunities of that office.

"So Benedict Musgrave is a member of the First Circle of Hecate?"

"He may or may not be," Symboline said with a smile. "But regardless, I am. And whenever I read cards for a querant, I am administering a sacrament, and it is privileged. We both know I don't have to answer any of your questions, detective."

"We can put you in front of a grand jury and you can answer theirs," Ouellette said.

"I don't think so. But you can try it. I got a brother-in-law who's a lawyer and he'd be all over this shit."

Lennox sighed.

"Ever get your cards read, detective?" she asked with a sly smile.

"No."

She took a worn tarot deck from a bag hanging at her belt. The cards were warped and discolored and sueded from years and years of use, from questions about lost loves and lost jobs, from *which?* and *what?* and *why?* From *will she?* to *why didn't he?* She caressed the old cards, shuffling and mixing them gracefully. She lifted half the pack and studied the card on the face of the packet for a long moment. A dead cut.

The Hermit.

In the garish Rider-Waite imagery, the card depicted a gray-cloaked figure with downcast eyes, a staff in one hand and a lantern on the other.

"Okay then," Lennox said. "Thanks for your time."

Symboline grinned.

"It's not quite what you think, detective," she said. "This is actually a really good card for you. The hermit is a seeker, but he must withdraw from the world, and first look within. He chooses Life over Death. When he makes his choice, he returns to the world as the Magician, as a man of power, of wisdom…"

She cut the cards again, and now held up the Magician card. A sleight-of-hand trick, Lennox was sure, but a good one.

"If you say so," he faltered. "If we have any other questions, we'll be in touch."

They followed her back into the shop. Symboline returned to the readers' room in back, and Lennox and Ouellette gently shouldered their way through the crush of customers. Out front, walking past the line of curious tourists, he muttered, "So that went well."

"Shut up."

Chapter XV

"**So where are we on this case?**" Winters asked irritably. "We've been on this for over a week, not counting your forty-eight hour surveillance request. Please tell me we have something."

"We have a dead body, identified as Charles Musgrave, son of Patience Musgrave, unmarried daughter the family had locked up in Danvers State Hospital," Ouellette said. "Our theory is that he came to Salem to get in touch with the family—possibly just to talk, but maybe to confront them and demand his share of the family fortune. And they killed him."

"Fabulous. Can you prove he contacted the family? Can you put him and them together?"

"We have the victim's cell phone records," Lennox said. Simpson of the Columbus PD had finally sent them over that morning. "Showing two calls to the family number, one on the night of Friday the sixteenth and the other the morning of the seventeenth. He was definitely in contact with them."

"Via phone. Can you place them together?"

"Possibly," Lennox said, not wanting to bring it up. "We have a potential witness who may have seen the dead man with a member of the family the day before the murder."

"A *potential* witness who *may* have seen them?" Winters asked. "What?"

Lennox quickly went over the story of his encounter with Danny, adding, "I still haven't heard anything back from the Danvers PD."

"A retarded witness in a graveyard in another jurisdiction? No. No no no. You bring me something else."

"Benedict, who we're thinking is our doer, was in the crowd when the body was found out at Gallows Hill," Lennox said.

"Which proves nothing other than that he was curious."

"The family clearly knows more than they're telling," Ouellette said.

"In your opinion."

"We also have an anonymous note, mailed to me, stating that the victim was killed in the house, and that there was proof in the family Bible."

"Do we know what that proof might consist of?" Winters began to gnaw on the end of a pencil.

"No idea. But along with the note, there was the missing key to the victim's car, which had been left in Beverly. So the note clearly comes from someone connected to the crime," Lennox said. "Someone in a position to know."

"Someone outside the family?"

"I don't think so."

"Who?"

"The mother and son present a united front, and I don't think they're going to budge without some serious evidence against them. On the other hand, Laura, the daughter our witness probably saw with the victim, is clearly more conflicted. I've seen her twice, and each time she seemed like she wanted to tell me something, desperately."

"Wait a minute," Winters said, taking the pencil from the corner of his mouth. "You've seen her twice? The initial contact and... when?"

"I bumped into her when I was out for a run," Lennox said quietly.

"No, you did not just *bump into her*, detective," Winters snapped. "You don't do that—you don't approach suspects outside the established parameters of a homicide investigation. Anything you found out could be ruled inadmissible. And it's just inappropriate. You know this."

Lennox nodded.

"So what's your next step?"

"I want a search warrant for the family home," Ouellette said. "We have reason to believe it's our primary crime scene, and we need to find the Bible. We have probable cause."

"I'll call the judge and hope she's in a good mood," Winters nodded.

A few hours later, Lennox and Ouellette once again stood on the Musgrave doorstep, this time with a search warrant in hand, as leaves swirled in a cool wind.

Harker and Foley stood just behind them, hands on holstered weapons. Johnson waited on the sidewalk with reinforcements from the state crime lab, impatient for the search to begin.

Ouellette did the knock-and-announce, banging on the door and then using the big brass knocker, calling, "This is Detective Sergeant Michelle Ouellette with the Salem Police Department. We are here to carry out a search warrant on this premises. Open the door. Now."

After a long moment, Laura Gagnon heaved the big door open.

"What's going on?" she asked. Her voice trembled as she blinked at the police gathered in front of the house. "Detective Lennox—what—?"

"What we want is clearly outlined in this search warrant," Ouellette said, pushing past her and into the hall. The others followed closely.

Lennox couldn't look Laura in the eye.

"Please step aside and do not interfere with the execution of the warrant," Ouellette went on in a forceful *don't-you-dare* deadpan. "If you do, you will be arrested. Where are your mother and your brother?"

"My mother is in the front parlor," Laura said, wrapping her arms around herself and stepping back against the wall. "Benedict... is out in the carriage house."

Ouellette nodded over to Lennox. He and a pair of uniformed officers went outside, rounding the corner of the house, and making their way across the broad, overgrown lawn to the carriage house out back.

The carriage house was a newer building than the family home, and was in poor repair. Paint flaked away from the old clapboards, and the roof was missing shingles. The main barn door was frozen shut with rust. The building seemed awkward and embarrassed next to the McIntire mansion standing nearby, so proud and aloof.

Lennox pounded on the Dutch door at one end of the building.

"Mr. Musgrave, this is Detective Lennox with the Salem PD. I need you to open the door."

A bleary Benedict Musgrave came to the door. He wore wrinkled khakis and a black t-shirt. His hair was uncombed and there was rough gray stubble on cheeks and chin. Lennox could tell that if the man had slept at all in the last few nights, he hadn't slept well. Over Benedict's shoulder, Lennox saw an old couch piled with blankets and quilts. One end of the couch was propped up with a cinder block. A card table at the other end was covered with empty beer bottles, greasy fast food wrappers, and a few of the dog-eared true crime paperbacks that Amanda Carson, nee Lewis, had found so creepy.

Benedict pulled on a sweater and scowled.

"What the hell is going on?"

"We're executing a search warrant," Lennox said. "Do you have any line out here, Benedict? Any diamond-braided polypropylene line?"

"What?"

"*Rope.* Do you have any *rope* out here?"

"No... I... no, no rope."

Lennox gestured to the two uniforms, who moved past Benedict and began searching the room.

"You're also looking for a leather cord," Lennox told them. He turned to Benedict. "I need you to come back to the house with me."

Benedict swore.

"I thought you said you lived upstairs?"

"I do."

"But you've been staying out here?" Lennox nodded past him, toward the couch. "Must get a little cold at night."

"I don't see that that's any of your goddamned business," Benedict said.

"So that's a yes, then," Lennox nodded, as he escorted him back to the main house.

Michelle Ouellette was the only still figure in the midst of the police personnel as Lennox came back onto the front parlor of the family mansion.

Johnson and her people had begun their preliminary walk-through before combing the house for evidence, warning others to be careful with what they were doing and shout if they found anything suspicious. Dworaczyk and other detectives arrived, along with another half dozen uniformed officers, and the small army was pulling the house apart. Out the window, a couple of news crews were setting up cameras across the street.

"Where is your family Bible?" Ouellette asked.

"What do you want with the Bible?" Agatha countered.

"The family Bible, now. That Bible," Ouellette stabbed a finger at the dour portrait of Silas Musgrave dominating the room. "Where is it? Now."

"It's there," Agatha said, indicating a Queen Anne bookstand across the room, all graceful wrought iron and teak. The great leather Bible was open to the Book of Exodus. Lennox bit his lip as he remembered *"Thou shalt not suffer a witch to live"* was somewhere in Exodus.

Ouellette nodded over to Johnson. "Bag it and tag it."

Johnson hefted the ancient book carefully. It probably weighed more than she did. She slid it gently into an evidence envelope, little leather curls flaking from the spine.

"Be careful!" Agatha shrieked across the room.

"We're moving you into another room while we get to work in here," Ouellette said to Agatha.

"Oh, the hell you are."

Ouellette gestured to one of the uniforms, and Agatha was abruptly wheeled from the room, swearing and threatening as she went.

Lennox pointed to Benedict and Laura.

"I need you two to come with me, please," he said.

"Where are we going?" Laura asked.

"I'm taking you both down to the station. With me. C'mon."

"Are we under arrest?"

"No. We just need to go over a few things with you, and we have too many people here already. So if you'll come with me…"

Lennox and a couple of uniforms walked out of the house, flanking the Musgrave siblings, as cameras flashed and the *Advertiser* and the *Argus* asked for a statement.

The brother and sister were placed in separate cruisers and driven to Margin Street. Lennox had already arranged for the car with Benedict to take the long way, and told the driver that hitting every pothole on the way might not be a bad idea.

Chapter XVI

LAURA ARRIVED AT THE STATION FIRST. She had never been so terrified in her life.

Once, when she was twenty, she had been pulled over for speeding, for doing thirty in a school zone. Broad green oak leaves had masked the speed limit signs, and the officer had let the pretty girl go with a warning. That had been her only encounter with the police.

Now, she sat in back of a cruiser headed for Margin Street, separated from the driver by a wire mesh cage. The driver, the striking blonde woman with the pentagram earrings, looked strangely familiar, and didn't say a word.

Terrified.

Lennox was there to meet her at the front door. She'd never even been inside a police station before. Big men with guns on their belts passed by her, nodding to Lennox, ignoring her. She cringed away from them, wincing from the slightest brush as they passed. Radios on their shoulders crackled and beeped, short cryptic messages being whispered back and forth. Once she heard the mansion's address spoken in a blur of static, and she couldn't stop her hands from shaking. He steered across the lobby to an interview room with a cold steel door.

Terrified.

"Am I under arrest?" she asked.

"No, nothing like that, Laura," Lennox said, shaking his head. "I just have a couple of questions. But before we start, is there anything you'd like to tell me? I thought the other day on the Common you wanted to say something. Did you?"

She almost violently shook her head, *no.*

He opened a folder and removed Paul Mather's driver's license photo.

"Okay, then. We'll start with Friday night. We have reason to believe that this man, calling himself Paul Mather, visited your family's home on Saturday the seventeenth. Have you ever seen him before?"

"No," she said, barely glancing at the photo. Lennox could tell she couldn't look. "Nobody came to the house. Nobody ever comes to the house."

"His name wasn't really Paul Mather, it was Charles Musgrave. He was the son of Patience Musgrave, your sister. She was a patient at Danvers State Hospital."

"I know who Patience was," she whispered.

"He came to the house on Saturday, and again on Sunday afternoon."

"I told you, nobody came to the house."

"On Saturday afternoon, you went to Danvers State with him. You visited Patience's grave."

"No. No, I have no idea what you are talking about."

"You were seen, and we'll get a statement from that witness. Your mother and Benedict planned this murder while you were out there with him."

"No."

"You had nothing to do with this murder, Laura. It's all your mother and your brother."

Lennox slid the anonymous note out of the folder and across the table.

Charles Musgrave was murdered in the family home on Sunday Oct. 18. The proof you need is in the family Bible.

"You sent this to me on Tuesday. Because you were trying to tell me something; you were trying to tell me what happened."

He took the key from the folder and placed it atop the note.

"You sent this along to prove you had first-hand knowledge of the crime. "

She was silent.

"We had a victim's body left in one location, and his car left elsewhere," he went on. "The murderer did things to the victim intended to confuse us—things like drawing pentagrams on his palms, and leaving him over at Gallows Hill. This close to Halloween, that made us look for a witchcraft connection, but it was just a red herring.

"Now the car was just left in a parking lot. No attempt at planting false evidence, no red herrings. Completely different style. So, two completely different people, one to dump the victim's body, one to get rid of the car. Benedict to dump the body, and you to get rid of the car. Right, Laura?"

Silence.

"When my dad was teaching me to drive—I was fifteen, and it was on an army base in Italy. When he taught me to drive, one thing he always said was *don't close the car door unless the keys are in your hand.* He always said that. Whoever taught you to drive told you the same thing, right, Laura? Because when you left that car in the parking lot, you got out and closed the door and you didn't even realize you still had the keys in your hand. You were on autopilot, you weren't thinking straight, because you didn't want any part of this. You couldn't believe what had just happened in that house—you'd seen your brother kill Charles, kill your nephew. Your own nephew."

"No, no, no—that didn't happen."

"You need to decide, right now, if you're going to be a witness, or a suspect. Talk to me, Laura. Let me help you."

Silence.

Even now, police asking questions in Salem were still shadowed by the legacy of three centuries before. Lennox could never interview a witness, never question a suspect, without the shades of those hysterical virgins and fire-and-brimstone magistrates looking over his shoulder, burdening him with their desperate zeal.

"Your brother is still under your mother's thumb. I've seen that. He lives in the family home, he never leaves. But you—you got out, you went to Barnard, you had four years in New York, and he's never left Salem. You have a husband, and a son, your own home. You've tried to get away from your family, from your family name, but I know how hard it is to break completely free. And even when something horrible happens, they're still the family. You couldn't come to me, so you reached out with this note, this key. I got the message, Laura. I need you to tell me the rest of what you're trying to say."

She opened her mouth to say something, but looked away and ground her lower lip with her expensively white teeth.

"What will we find in the Bible, Laura?"

Nothing.

"Laura? You've made some bad mistakes here, and this might be your only chance to clear things up. Let me help you."

"It's very cold in here," she said in a small, distant voice.

And he knew that he had lost her.

He got up from the table and closed the door behind him as he left the room, feeling awful in more ways than he could count.

Leaving the others to continue their searches downstairs, Ouellette climbed the broad staircase to the second floor. Benedict said he lived down the hall, indicating the ground floor, and the invalid Agatha would probably not be negotiating a flight of stairs at least twice a day, so Ouellette was uncertain of what she might find.

It was cooler up here, almost cold, and less claustrophobic, but the air was stale, smelling of dust and age and neglect. The rooms were arranged symmetrically down the length of a high-ceilinged corridor, with a heavily-draped window at the far end; the sunlight barely penetrated here. A narrower, steeper staircase led up to the third floor, to the servants' quarters.

She checked each of the rooms, and one after another was empty, unused. The rooms were large and would have been comfortable had they been furnished, had there been any sign of life. But there was nothing. Just a series of forgotten rooms and shuttered windows. As she turned, she saw her own faint footprints on the dusty floor.

No one had been up here in years.

Carefully ascending the servants' stairs to the top floor, she used her flashlight to light the way. If the second floor was dim, the third was dark. Floorboards creaked under her step as she shone the light into the corners of the little, monastic rooms up here. She reached out a few times, feeling for light switches that weren't there.

Empty, cold rooms again, one after another after another.

Bizarre.

The stairs were slippery with dust as she made her way back down to the second floor. Motes eddied in the sunlight as she threw open the drapes at the end of the hall. She wondered when the curtains had last been open. Months? Years? Decades?

"Sergeant," Johnson called from the ground floor. "We're ready to start spraying down here."

In the front parlor, Johnson closed the shutters and pulled the drapes under the harsh scowl of Silas Musgrave. The room became surprisingly dark. Ouellette and Dworaczyk stood in the doorway as Johnson took a spray bottle of Luminol from her kit.

"Any place in particular you want me to start?" she asked.

Ouellette shook her head and Johnson began with the walls, working her way around the room, spraying up and down as she went, looking for the telltale blue-white glow that indicated the presence of blood. A photographer followed a step behind.

It took her twenty minutes to complete checking the walls. Nothing.

She turned her attention to the floor, starting with the area by the hearth and moving out across the room from there. Halfway between the fireplace and the big Queen Anne table, the floor lit up in ghostly blue splashes and streaks.

"Got it!" Dworaczyk said.

"That's not blood," Johnson sighed. "That's bleach."

Chlorine bleach reacted with Luminol and produced the same chemiluminescence as blood, hiding whatever bloodstains there might be. It was the kind of thing a person who read true crime paperbacks would know. Johnson was not happy.

"Someone cleaned the hell out of the scene," Dworaczyk murmured.

"So there's no rug, obviously, but we did lift a few fibers from the floor," Johnson said. "The problem is that they were so damaged by the bleach that I seriously doubt we can match them to the rug fibers we found on the body."

"What about the candlesticks over there?" Ouellette asked.

Johnson sprayed and said, "Goddamn bleach again."

Ouellette hefted one of the candlesticks. Heavy. Well balanced for swinging.

"This is our murder weapon," she said. "Why clean antique silver with bleach unless you're trying to get rid of blood evidence?"

"A defense attorney will give you a list of reasons," Dworaczyk said.

"The square base would fit the wounds…"

"And so would nearly anything else with a right angle," Johnson countered.

"Look, you and I both know this is our scene, and this is our weapon. But it is all circumstantial. We cannot prove a damn thing here," Dworaczyk said. "And juries, they like their proof."

"Not helping," Ouellette said, but she knew they were right. "Either of you."

Two blister packs of Xanax were still in his right-hand desk drawer upstairs, under some empty file folders. Twenty pills. Lennox could almost taste them, almost feel the bitter grit the tablet made when he swallowed one just a little too slowly. He didn't have time to run back to the bullpen—Benedict was waiting in the other interview room. He'd had Benedict brought in through booking, buzzed through locked doors, through metal detectors, past the holding cells with drunk tourists sleeping off benders, and sullen-eyed townies with blank expressions.

Plunkett had been waiting in one corner of the interview room. He'd nodded, told Benedict that Lennox would be with him shortly, and didn't say another word, writing and writing instead on a yellow legal pad balanced on one knee. This was an old tactic to make the suspect nervous, and Plunkett did it better than anyone. Lennox knew that whatever the man was writing had nothing to do with Benedict, and might not even be in English. Plunkett was old enough to remember the Latin Mass, and paused briefly to eye Benedict searchingly in between writing out the *sanctus* and the *libera nos*.

"Sorry to keep you waiting," Lennox said insincerely when he finally arrived. Benedict had been stewing, and Plunkett had been writing, for over an hour.

Benedict sat against the far wall, behind a table bolted to the floor. He rose to his feet, up to his full height, a head taller, throwing his chest out. He scowled. Alpha male. Prize fighter. Not afraid of you.

"So this is an interrogation?" he asked with a bitter smirk.

Lennox smiled patiently. He had FBI certification in interrogation techniques, and taught seminars at the police academy. If this were an official interrogation, he'd make damn sure Benedict knew it.

"Just need to go over a few things. So I noticed a stack of true crime paperbacks in the carriage house," Lennox began, taking a seat and opening the case file. He sorted through the reports and photos. "Ever go over to the Black Museum? It's on Derby. It's all displays of famous criminals and their crimes."

"Never been."

"I actually own the place," he smiled. "Plunkett's there all the time."

"Can't get enough of that place," Plunkett said, not looking up from his pad.

"So, you're the good cop, then," Benedict said sullenly. "Am I even under arrest?"

"We're just talking. Last weekend, a man claiming to be Charles Musgrave showed up on the doorstep. Charles was the son of your sister Patience. You were still a kid when all this happened, but your mother had him adopted out years ago and tried to forget all about him. But now the prodigal heir has returned and this is a serious problem—he's asking about what happened to his mother. He's asking about what *Agatha did* to his mother all those years ago. Even worse, he's asking about his inheritance, the trust fund Agatha stole."

"Nobody came to the house—"

"The money is long gone. Agatha's freaked out. She needs time to think about what the hell to do," Lennox interrupted, holding up a warning finger. "So she puts him off, tells him to come back Sunday. For tea and scones. She tells him we'll work everything out then. But she already knows. She can't let him live. So she orders his execution. An execution to be carried out by you, Benedict. You tried to strangle him."

He slapped three morgue photos down on the table. Rusty ligature marks against Charles Musgrave's pallid throat.

"But he got away from you. Gave you that shiner," he gestured to the yellow stain lingering under Benedict's right eye. "So you bashed him over the head. Five times. A couple of times once he was down. But now that he's dead, you have a whole new set of problems. Like getting rid of the body, getting rid of the antique rug he'd bled all over."

"This is all—"

"*You'll get your turn.* Now, your nephew was adopted by a family named Mather, which is about the worst possible name for someone to have here in town. But it gave you a hell of an idea, didn't it? Finding the body of a man named Mather hanging at Gallows Hill would make us ask all the wrong questions, send us down all the wrong paths. But why stop there? Those pentagrams on the palms—"

More photos slapped down on the table. Green sharpie marker on white flesh.

Silence.

"God, I feel so bad for you, Benedict. I really do. You had nothing to do with this. Nothing. You didn't lock Patience up, you didn't steal her money. That's all Agatha. You had nothing to do with any of that. You probably didn't even know who the hell this guy was until she told you. But when Charles showed up, she tells you to clean it up—she tells you to kill him. You live in her house, she gives the orders. You did what you were told to do."

Benedict opened his mouth, and seemed to think about it before closing it.

"She put you up to this," Lennox said simply.

"I didn't kill anyone."

"You were home Sunday, though."

"Well, yeah."

"So you were home then but nothing happened."

"Right…"

"This guy wasn't there."

"No."

"But you were," Plunkett said.

"Right."

"But you didn't kill him."

"No. I didn't kill anybody."

"You were ready to kill James Carson, though. After he—what was the word—*stole* Amanda? They had to take out a restraining order."

Benedict licked his lips and leaned back in the chair.

"You found out about that?"

"I find out about everything, Benedict."

"I… might have said something like that, but that was a long time ago, but…"

"But what?"

"But threatening someone is a long way from killing them."

"Not as far as you'd think. And you did punch Mr. Carson. That gives you what we like to call *a history of violence.*"

Silence.

"Maybe we've been looking at this the wrong way the whole time," Lennox said. "Maybe Charles Musgrave came in demanding his inheritance—or else. He took a swing at you—that's what started all this. He threatened your mother, he threatened Laura. He hit you and it all just exploded from there, didn't it? It just went completely out of control. Those ligature marks, we assumed they were from an attempted strangulation, but they could have been post-mortem, could have been from hanging him up from that tree. We weren't quite sure and really, the lab gets stuff like that wrong all the time."

"Am I under arrest?"

"Not yet."

"Then you don't have anything. If you did, you'd arrest me," Benedict said, hauling himself to his feet. "I'm leaving."

Lennox rose and leaned in close, lowering his voice.

"Benedict, we have a forensics team going over every inch of your house, okay? And they're paying very, very close attention to that family Bible. And once they find what they're looking for, then we just start charging you all with murder. This is your only chance, Benedict. Right here, right now. Talk to me. You walk out that door, and…"

"I'm leaving."

"Why have you been camped out in the carriage house? Mom throw you out? After that argument last Saturday?"

"I said I'm leaving."

"Who is Eric Scully? What did he want?"

"What?" Benedict asked.

"Eric Scully, the man who tried to break into your house. Who is he?

"My God, you people don't know anything, do you?"

Benedict moved around the table and shambled to the door, pulling at the handle, and out into the lobby, where Laura waited for him on a bench. He didn't even see her, and she rose to follow as he walked stiffly past. Lennox gestured to the uniforms to let them go.

Ouellette would still be interviewing the old woman at the house. He flipped open his cell and texted her.

L & B released. No joy.

He put the phone away and looked up at the tiny video camera tucked into the tall corner by the door. He shrugged, knowing that Winters was upstairs in the Major Case Room, watching the monitor with disapproval.

He went up to the bullpen, exhausted, grabbing for the right-hand drawer of his desk.

Chapter XVII

THE FORENSICS REPORTS ARRIVED LATE the next day. It took nearly an hour for Lennox and Ouellette to go over it all. The crime scene report spent several pages explaining that they had discovered no useful evidence in the family home. Lennox was particularly disappointed as he read that no rope had been found, and that the front parlor had been bleached, damaging the rug fibers they'd discovered.

"I thought I smelled bleach the first time we interviewed the family."

"I got a whiff of it, too," Ouellette said. "At least we finally know where our crime scene is."

"We know he was killed there because of a complete lack of evidence indicating he was killed there," Lennox said absently. He turned to Johnson's report on the Bible.

It was a Geneva Bible, the first generally available edition of the Scripture, predating the King James translation by half a century. This particular copy was a 1599 edition. A massive leather book that barely fit in the evidence envelope, thousands of pages of close packed script. The first Bible to divide chapters into verses, a Geneva Bible was among the texts brought to the New World aboard the *Mayflower* and was the edition that Shakespeare and Milton would have known.

Johnson's background research was always so thorough.

She and the experts on loan from the state crime lab had spent hours going through the book one page at a time, using a variety of lenses, lights, and filters, checking for telltale marks, smudges, fingerprints, the slightest trace of trace evidence. She checked for signatures, and secret ciphers, hidden messages. And in the end, she had submitted a lengthy report, filled with charts and graphs and formulae, saying that she had found nothing.

"Well, at least we made the front page." Lennox said, picking up a copy of the *Argus*. The headline read *Police Raid Historic Home*. The photo showed Lennox, flanked by a pair of uniformed officers, outside on the Musgrave doorstep. He scowled at the camera, having noticed it only an instant before the photo was snapped. *Dammit,* he thought.

The article described the police entering the house with warrants, the search, the detectives and officers coming and going over several hours. One unnamed officer had apparently spoken briefly with a reporter and admitted the dead man found at Gallows Hill two weeks ago had been a relative of the family. That made Ouellette swear quietly in French. Whoever had talked to the reporters would regret it if Ouellette found out who it was.

"Above the fold, too," he noted ruefully. "And there was no raid; it was a search. Doesn't anyone know the difference anymore? At least they got my good side."

Ouellette managed a tight, unhappy smile.

"So you're the primary; what's the next move?"

"Find out who talked to the reporter and have him writing parking tickets, to begin with," she said. "We have nothing on these people. Just suspicions and speculations."

"Which add up."

"We need physical evidence."

The phone on his desk rang.

"CID, Lennox."

"Detective," a velvety female voice said, "Please hold for Mr. Maitland."

"I'm sorry, who is—"

"Hello, Detective, this is Christopher Maitland," came a dry voice. Something in the tone indicated he expected Lennox to recognize the name. "I've been following the news reports of the murder you're investigating."

"Yes?"

"I'm in Boston—can you meet me tomorrow? We should talk."

"And what do we have to talk about, Mr. Maitland?"

"The murdered man… Charles Musgrave."

"Yes?"

"He was my son."

"We can be in Boston by nine tomorrow," Lennox said, smiling over at Ouellette.

Both Lennox and Ouellette hated driving in Boston, so they took a commuter train, jammed into a car with seemingly every North Shore resident who worked in the city.

Ouellette had looked up Christopher Maitland the night before; given half an hour and an internet connection, there seemed to be few things she could not find out. She was following up a few leads on her smartphone now, as Lennox watched Swampscott and Lynn roll by.

Maitland was president and CEO of Maitland Construction/Development, the sprawling offices of which looked out over the Boston skyline. Falling just short of the Fortune 500 list, MC/D still employed thousands to build hospitals, highways, and corporate skyscrapers up and down the east coast. In interviews, Maitland loved recounting his up-from-nothing story, how as a teenager in a bad neighborhood in Salem he had made two thousand dollars one summer, painting garages and sealing driveways. Knowing he wouldn't get rich in the Witch City, he left town to make his way in the wider world and within a decade, he had traded his work boots for wingtips and presided over a company with half a dozen divisions and national recognition. Now he was well-known as a philanthropist who sat on the boards of various charities and foundations and lived with his wife and children in various homes scattered around New England.

But several years ago, he had nearly lost everything. Union complaints and strikes, along with budget overruns and accusations of bribing public officials and hiring battalions of undocumented workers hit the company hard. Being part of Boston's unpopular Big Dig, with its own accusations of mismanagement and corruption, didn't help, and the financial meltdown only made everything worse. Shareholders called for Maitland's ouster and he had to fight to keep control of the company he had built brick by brick. He eventually won out after months of boardroom warfare, and it took over a year for him to rehab his reputation, and now he coyly dodged rumors that he was planning a run for public office—city council, if not actually mayor. Popular opinion was that he'd win hands down.

The detectives took a cab from the train station to an office building in the North End, where MC/D took up an entire floor. The elevator seemed to take forever, and a sleek secretary silently guided them down a long corridor when they said Mr. Maitland was expecting them.

Maitland himself was a tall and thin, tan, with thick salt and pepper hair, ten years older than he looked, probably. He wore a tailor-made dark suit, no tie, and smiled a perfect white smile as Lennox and Ouellette entered his office. He had a firm handshake.

"Please, have a seat," he gestured to a pair of leather chairs next to the broad expanse of his desk. "Coffee should be in in just a moment."

"Thank you," Lennox said, as he and Ouellette took seats.

A giant photo took up most of one wall in Maitland's office— a closeup of a carved wooden eagle, gold feathers, red eyes, and a hooked beak.

"That's the Custom House eagle," Lennox said.

"Very good, detective," Maitland nodded. "I used to pass by the Custom House nearly every day growing up in town." He gestured approvingly at the photo. "Joseph True was the best woodcarver in Salem not named Samuel McIntire."

"You said you'd been following news coverage of the investigation," Ouellette said, trying to get them on track. "The case has gotten more media attention that we would have liked."

"You said you were Charles's father?" Lennox asked.

"Yes. That was a lifetime ago…" Maitland said quietly.

"Were you in contact with him?"

"No. Never."

"He didn't reach out to you once he arrived in Massachusetts?"

"No."

"How did you meet Patience?"

"She met me, so to speak," he smiled wistfully; Lennox knew he was seeing the image of his pretty sixteen-year-old girlfriend in his mind. "She was something of a wild child. She drank, she smoked, she ran around with boys. Always going places she shouldn't, getting herself into trouble. Her family was not happy—Musgraves did not behave that way," he chuckled at some private memory. "But Patience did. Our paths crossed a few times, we noticed one another, and then one night she asked if I had a cigarette… and there we were."

Lennox nodded. Patience, the wild child who gave the retarded kid her red jello. The wild child who was secretly a good kid.

"Did she bring you home to meet the family?" Ouellette asked.

"Hardly. I wasn't the sort of boy you bring home to mother—especially to Agatha. My parents were divorced, I grew up in a bad neighborhood, never had clean clothes, was always getting into fights with the Spanish kids around town, back when they still taught boxing at the Y. There are probably a few other things I shouldn't get into with a couple of police detectives," he chuckled warmly. "No, she could never introduce me to the family. But she did sneak me into the house a few times. I had never seen anything like it! I couldn't believe people actually lived like that. Completely mind blowing to an eighteen-year-old kid from the wrong side of the tracks." He shook his head. "It was a different world.

"I dodged Agatha. I met Benedict, who probably would have warned me to stay away from his sister if the family had given a damn about her. Laura was terrified of me, but she and Patience were thick as thieves."

Another sleek secretary brought coffee on a silver tray. She was almost indistinguishable from the woman who had greeted them in the lobby. Maitland must have a type, Lennox thought.

"After Patience got pregnant and Agatha sent her to Danvers," Ouellette said.

"Yes…"

"What happened there?" she asked.

"Well, old Uncle Charles died, and then Patience realized she was pregnant. That sent the family onto a frenzy—they knew about the terms of his will, you see."

"But Uncle Charles's will named his college roommate as his heir," Lennox said, paging far back in the notebook of his organizer. "One George Linnell."

"Yes, but he was killed. You knew that, didn't you?"

"Car accident."

Christopher Maitland smiled bitterly.

"No accident."

"Really? Agatha?"

"Agatha. She realized that one life stood between Patience and all that money. Eyewitnesses said that a dark blue car ran the man down as he crossed the street. It didn't happen far from here, as a matter of fact. Would you care to guess what kind of car Agatha drove back then, detective?"

"A dark blue one?."

"And with that obstacle out of the way, Patience was now heir to a fortune," Maitland went on. "And Agatha got her troublesome daughter locked away and got control of the trust. Two birds, one stone."

"But Patience contested it—in her guardianship file, I found paperwork from two different doctors stating that Patience was fully competent and should be released."

"Two doctors who never practiced medicine again after making that recommendation," Maitland said.

"You're kidding."

"You cannot overestimate the power, or the reach, of the Musgrave name back then. Agatha made a few calls, the doctors lost their licenses, and soon it was understood…"

"Don't go near the Musgrave girl or the family will destroy your career," Ouellette nodded.

"Exactly, detective."

"What a nice family."

"They make the Borgias look like amateurs," Maitland chuckled.

"Agatha seems very wrapped up in preserving the ancient Musgrave family name," Lennox said. "It's a lot of crazy effort for a family she married into."

"Ah, detective. You didn't look into the genealogy then, did you?"

"Not… extensively," Lennox said, hating to admit it.

"Agatha is a Musgrave. She and Phillip were cousins."

As Amanda Lewis had said, the family was very eighteenth century about things.

"Okay… so when Patience was in Danvers, what did you do?"

"I couldn't do anything. I was a teenager, we weren't married, I wasn't given as the father on Charles's birth certificate—they never would have listed my name in any event, not back then. Only the family was allowed to visit her, not that any of them did, of course." He sighed, the sorrow from all those years ago seeming to catch up with him suddenly on this sunny autumn morning, decades later. "I heard that she gave birth to our son, and that Agatha quickly put him up for adoption and that was the end of it."

"How did you hear about it?"

"Laura. She was so happy that her big sister was going to have a baby. Poor Laura, I think she thought Patience was going to come home again—that she went to the hospital to have the baby and would come back home after. She didn't understand the family was never going to let that happen. But eventually she realized big sister was staying there, and the baby was gone… she didn't take the news well. She was so angry…"

"And you left town."

"Again, the Musgraves were a powerful family back then. They were able to make it very… unwelcoming. I spent a summer painting garages and saving my pennies and got out of town."

He sighed and sipped his coffee thoughtfully. Lennox and Ouellette gave him a few moments, and waited for him to speak again.

"So, detectives, where are you in your investigation of my son's murder?" he asked after a long while.

"We're following up on some very promising leads, and have been making steady progress." Ouellette said.

"No you haven't," said Christopher Maitland. It was a simple comment, and he half-smiled as he made it. "My son was killed two weeks ago and you still haven't made an arrest. You finally searched the Musgrave home yesterday and apparently came up with empty-handed. My son's body has undoubtedly been buried in Ohio and you have done *nothing*."

"We really can't comment on an ongoing investigation."

"It's not ongoing. You've hit a brick wall. You know they're guilty. Agatha is an old woman, Laura is spineless, Benedict is the only one who could have… killed Charles. At Agatha's behest."

"We'll bear that in mind," Ouellette said.

"I would be only too happy to see the Musgrave family pay for their many, many sins," Maitland said quietly. "Not the least of which is the murder of my son. I am not without resources. If I can be of any assistance… I know sometimes official channels can be… slow-moving. Sometimes those of us in the private sector, especially those of us with certain connections, can get results more expeditiously, and more discreetly."

"We appreciate the offer," Ouellette said politely. "We still have some work to do today and we shouldn't really take up any more of your time, Mr. Maitland. Thank you for meeting with us this morning."

"One last thing, detectives," Maitland said as they rose to go. "I have a wife, I have children, and I have a successful career and a reputation…"

"And you'd like us to keep your name out of it if we can," Ouellette said.

"Patience was my first love," he said quietly. "What happened to her was horrible, and there was nothing I could do about it. But I can't really have it known that I got a sixteen-year-old girl pregnant when I was just a teenager."

"Especially if you're considering a run for office," Lennox said.

Maitland nodded slowly, without meeting the detectives' gaze. He had fought his way back from the brink once before, they realized, and didn't want to risk another fight

"No promises," Ouellette said.

The Common Burying Point, Cotton Mather's final resting place, visited one night by one of Harker's angry friends, was only a few blocks from Maitland's building. Lennox wanted to visit the grave, being so nearby, but Ouellette vetoed it.

On the way back to the train, Ouellette noticed that Lennox had that face again. Something was on his mind.

"What are you thinking?"

"Is it just me, or did he seem to want something?"

"Yes. He wanted to know if we had arrested his son's killer."

"Well, yeah, but there was something else."

"He wanted us to keep his name out of it."

"Right, but beyond all that. He wanted something. He wasn't going to come right out and say it, but he wanted something."

Ouellette's phone beeped.

"Ouellette. Yes?" She glanced over to Lennox. "Yes, sir. We're in Boston following up a lead. We're just getting on the train back. Why?"

She listened and bit her lip.

"*Merde.* We'll be there as soon as we can."

"What was that?" Lennox asked as she slid the phone back into her pocket.

"Winters. Laura Gagnon is in the hospital. She just tried to kill herself." She sighed. "*Tabarnak.*"

Chapter XVIII

AN HOUR LATER, Lennox and Ouellette arrived at North Shore Medical Center. A uniformed officer stood outside of Laura Gagnon's room.

"What the hell happened?" Lennox asked before Ouellette could.

"10-56A call came in at 10:40 a.m. Her husband went off to work and then came back, says he forgot something, and found her lying on the floor. Looks like she took everything in the medicine cabinet. They pumped her stomach but she still hasn't woken up. And I heard them saying they aren't sure how functional she'll be if she ever does."

Ouellette quietly swore in French again.

"Husband's in there with her," the uniform added.

Ouellette and Lennox entered the room and closed the door quietly behind them.

Laura Musgrave Gagnon lay propped up on the hospital bed. The room was dark. Tubes and wires snaked into the shadows, connecting her to machines with cryptic screens and weird readouts glowing in the gloom. The machines beeped ominously. She looked as pale as her nephew had when they found him hanging in Gallows Hill Park.

Neil Gagnon sat in a chair by his wife's bedside, his fingers laced with hers, his hair disheveled, his tie pulled loose. It was barely noon and he already looked exhausted, and he probably was.

"Mr. Gagnon?" Ouellette asked quietly.

He startled, unaware they had entered.

"Yes?"

"I'm Detective Sergeant Ouellette, and this is Detective Lennox."

Gagnon nodded and, as he made the connection, shifted his gaze over to Lennox, still standing just inside the door.

"She spoke with you on the Common, she mentioned it," he said thickly.

Lennox nodded.

"Then you brought her in for questioning..."

"We're in the middle of a murder investigation," Lennox replied. "We've questioned a number of people."

"And how many of those people try to kill themselves after you question them, detective?" he asked in a harsh whisper.

"Mr. Gagnon, I know this must be hard for you. But your wife was trying to tell me something. Something important—"

"She didn't have anything to say to you. You scared the hell out of her, just happening to bump into her on the Common and then hauling her down to the station a couple of days later. Why were you harassing her?"

"I was not harassing her. I was conducting an investigation."

"Get the fuck out of here. I don't want you *near* her."

Lennox gave Ouellette an *I'll-wait-for-you-outside* nod and let the door close behind him as he went.

"Mr. Gagnon, if my partner is right, and if she was trying to tell us something, do you have any idea what it might have been?" she asked.

"You honestly think she had something to do with that murder?"

"We think she must know something about it," Ouellette corrected gently.

"That whole family is a mess," Neil Gagnon said, running a nervous hand over his face. "I don't doubt that they might have... done something, but Laur had nothing to do with it. She's the only normal one in that whole sick family, I swear to God. She spends a lot of time at the old house, but she can't really talk to them.

Agatha is very controlling. Crazy old bitch. God, that family. She wants nothing to do with them, but she can't get away from them, you know? Sometimes, she wants to get as far away from them as she can—away from them, from the family name, from Salem… but she just can't."

Nobody ever left Salem.

"She couldn't have had anything to do with that man's death."

"That man was her nephew," Ouellette said. "They were seen together. How has she been the past few weeks? Has she seemed okay to you?"

She made sure to speak of Laura in the present tense.

"No," he said sadly. "I mean, she was upset about the whole thing, about you people waving around search warrants and asking questions. And then following her around for a few days."

Laura had spotted the surveillance. Clever girl.

"All part of a homicide investigation, Mr. Gagnon. We were eliminating her from our suspect pool," she said, the standard response to such complaints.

He shook his head angrily.

"Did she say anything about what was going on?"

"She wouldn't talk about it, not with me."

"Who would she have talked to?"

"No one," he said sadly.

Ouellette stood awkwardly by the bed, not sure what to say next. Lennox was so much better with people than she was.

"Here's my card," Ouellette held it out, then left it on the edge of the table when he didn't even acknowledge it. "I know this is a bad time for you, but if you think of anything, or if I can be of help in some way, please get in touch."

He probably wasn't even aware of her leaving the room.

When they finished reporting in to Winters back at the station, the Lieutenant dismissed Ouellette and asked Lennox to stay.

"Andrew, I'm taking you off this case," he said.

"What?" Lennox asked, although he had known this was coming. He had spent the train ride back from Boston knowing this would happen.

"About five minutes after he got to the hospital, Neil Gagnon called me, and he wanted your head on a pike," Winters explained patiently. Very patiently. "He said that the actions of this department, and of you in particular, constitute harassment, and he'd be talking to his lawyers. Lawyers. Plural."

Lennox could only shake his head.

"He said his wife would never have done what she did if you hadn't stalked her to the Common—yes, he said stalked—and then hauled her in for questioning."

"There was no hauling, and there sure as hell wasn't any stalking."

"But there were stupid mistakes, Andrew. I have to take you off of this. The investigation is stalled anyway. I'm going to assign Dworaczyk to work with Ouellette, and to be honest, if she doesn't make headway this week, I'll take her off it, too."

No, you won't, he thought.

One of the many things that annoyed him when watching cop shows was how officers talked back to their superiors, yelled at them. Growing up in a military family, three tours in the Coast Guard, and nine years on the job had taught him about hierarchy, about chain of command. It had taught him how to nod and say, "Yes, sir."

"You're off, effective immediately. You were never supposed to be on this case to begin with, dammit. Work on closing Paiva."

Ouellette saw Lennox come out of Winters's office and stumble across the bullpen. He took something small from the right-hand drawer of his desk, slamming it shut, shoving whatever it was into a coat pocket and leaving without a word. She watched him go.

"Fred," Winters called to Dworaczyk. "You will now be assisting Sergeant Ouellette on the Musgrave case. Have her bring you up to speed."

Dworaczyk rose, straightened his tie, and crossed the bullpen with a satisfied swagger. Taking a seat next to her desk, he asked, "So, Michelle, where do you want to start?"

"It's theater," he said to Morrow the next day. The little fountain with the fake river stones was particularly distracting today. Disturbing, even. "It's a show for the lawyers. Plural. So he can throw up his hands and tell Gagnon that he's reassigned me. I understand why Winters is doing it, but... I can't understand why he's doing it." He leaned forward, head in his hands. He felt like he was going to be sick. "They think I drove her to it. Like I hadn't already been thinking that. So I'm off the case, and she might never wake up."

"You can't blame yourself for another's actions, Andrew," Dr. Morrow said.

"Maybe I did push her a little hard," Lennox said. "Maybe I should have recognized... I don't know anymore."

"So put that aside for now, Andrew. It's out of your control. You need to refocus your attention on something where you are in control."

"She might never wake up," he said.

Chapter XIX

HE SPENT THE NEXT MORNING at the firing range, emptying clip after clip into target silhouettes and cutouts. He'd always had good aim. His accuracy in throwing a hauling line back in the Coast Guard translated to accuracy with firearms, and he was rated as a marksman in the department. There was something oddly relaxing about it, giving himself over to the simple repetition of loading, aiming, firing, reloading, aiming, firing. Letting the muscle memory take over and shunt him through the practiced actions, was almost Zen, he thought idly. But then again, he was firing off round after round at human-shaped paper targets, so perhaps it was more Freudian.

His cell phone rang as he left the station.

"Detective Lennox? It's Danielle Mather."

He felt a knot in his stomach.

"Have you made any progress? Do you know what... happened to him? To Paul?"

"We're still working on it," he said lamely. "*They're* still working on it," he corrected.

"What do you mean?"

"I've actually been... transferred to another case for right now."

"So you aren't working on Paul's murder?"

"Our best people are on it," he said, feeling like an insincere politician dodging a question. "They're doing everything they can. There are a couple of things they're following up on, and I think you'll be hearing good news from them in a couple of days."

"What are they doing? Do they have a suspect?"

"It's… not my case anymore," he said. It never really had been, of course. It had been Ouellette's. But she'd brought him in, knowing how much he needed to work. "So I can't really go into it with you. You should call the station and ask for Detective Sergeant Ouellette."

"Okay," Danielle Mather sighed.

"I'm… I'm sorry."

He wanted to throw up.

Salem State University's main campus was on the south side of the city. Lennox had spent probably fifteen minutes on the phone tracking down Professor Peter Prescott, being transferred and forwarded almost endlessly before finally reaching the man.

"I can meet you at one o'clock," Prescott had said. "You'll never find my office on campus, so why don't we meet in front of the library?"

Lennox didn't usually allow the subject to set the time and place for a meeting, but he'd agreed, and at ten minutes to one he was standing outside the library.

The very thought of setting foot on the SSU campus made him queasy. The fact that Ellen taught there, had left him for someone there, gave the place a weird lion's den quality.

He'd met her in college, shortly after he'd disappointed his career-military parents by not signing up. He hadn't been sure what he wanted to do, he just knew the army wasn't for him. Let them pin their hopes on his brother. After graduation he did three tours with the Coast Guard while Ellen pursued her masters and then her doctorate. Allison's arrival three years after their marriage had been a surprise, and as he watched her begin to grow up, time away on an icebreaker or chasing drug smugglers lost its appeal. He wanted to be home more. With his family. They settled in Boston, moving to Salem a year later when he graduated the police academy, his dozen years in the Coast Guard sending him to the front of the line of job applicants. Ellen easily netted a teaching job at SSU.

Where she met Martin Frazier. He taught in the history department, offering courses titled *Firebrands of Hell: Deconstructing "Hysteria"*, and *Salem Possessed: Witchtrial as Culturewar*. Because in Salem, it seemed that no one could get very far from the witch trials. And that was partially, if not largely, by choice.

Lennox and Frazier had gotten along well enough, seeing one another at the obligatory gatherings where he was Ellen's husband, the cop. Frazier was tall and thin and tweedy, with a small mustache and round glasses. But Lennox soon noticed a strange reserve, a kind of stand-offish quality when he saw Frazier. A distancing. And it finally made sense one night, when Ellen came home late and told him that, after being married for seventeen years, after raising a daughter together, she was leaving him. For Martin Frazier.

The detective who hadn't seen it coming.

This campus was the last place he wanted to be right now. He tucked a Xanax under his tongue, waiting for it to slowly dissolve. He pulled his cap down low on his forehead, shoving his hands deep in his pockets. He tried not to startle, tried not to think that every woman he glimpsed out of the corner of his eye was his ex-wife.

And campus was busy. Midterms were a week away, but most students had their sights set on tomorrow night—Halloween. SSU always had a reputation as a party school, and the parties, kegger and costume, had been going on all week. There were even rumors of a kegger where costumes were completely optional, wink wink nudge nudge. He'd let the campus police handle that one. Students flowed by, many in costumes and painted faces already—skulls, the inevitable green-faced witches in tiny black dresses, blond-wigged Vikings, the school mascot—all shuffling through the wet leaves scattered across the quad. Plastic jack-o-lanterns in pointed witch hats sat on the library windows—Lennox wondered if they were there year round, though he wasn't sure he remembered them from the handful of law enforcement classes he'd once taken when they first arrived in Salem.

"Dad?"

His head snapped up. Allison.

"Hey there," he said, trying to sound nonchalant, and knowing how badly he wasn't.

"What are you doing here?" she asked, glancing around a little nervously.

"I'm meeting someone," he replied, looking at his watch. "He's late."

"Everyone meets in front of the library," she said. "It's a thing. Who are you meeting?"

"Professor Prescott."

She nodded. She had cut her hair since he had seen her last—and when was that? He couldn't remember. Her hair had been down past her shoulders, and now stopped at her chin. She still wore the jeans and the corduroy man's jacket she'd always liked, but there was nothing of the tomboy about her at all. It always surprised him to realize just how much she looked like her mother, and each time he wondered how he could have possibly forgotten that.

"What do you need to see him about?"

"You know him?"

"I've heard of him," she shrugged. "I see him around."

"It's for a case."

"Oh," she said quietly, knowing better than to ask further.

Her phone rang. She pulled it from her pocket and glanced at the caller ID screen. She smiled awkwardly at Lennox before taking a step back, and answering with a forced *"Hi!"*

She looked back over to her father before saying, "Yeah, I'm already out front. Yeah. Um… Dad's here. Yeah. He says it's for a case. Okay. See you in a bit."

"So you're meeting Mom?"

He wondered vaguely if he could take another Xanax without her noticing.

"Everyone meets in front of the library," she smiled. "It's a thing."

"Except me and Professor Prescott, apparently," he said, glancing around him. His watch showed one-fifteen. Dammit. Ellen would get here before this guy did. He just knew it. "So, um... listen."

He paused. This really wasn't a conversation he wanted to have with his daughter. He nodded toward the people passing by the library, coming up and down the steps and zigzagging their way across the campus.

"So... I know it must be against the rules, but I'm sure it happens anyway. Do any teachers here get... involved with their students?"

Allison's face flushed, embarrassed.

"I wouldn't say a lot," she said uncomfortably. "I mean, I don't think anyone's keeping numbers on it or anything. But yeah, it happens. It's not officially against the rules—they figure if it's not a problem, it's not a problem, you know? So, it happens."

"Please tell me you aren't speaking from experience," he smirked.

"Not yet," she smirked back.

"Not funny."

"So that's why you're here for Professor Prescott."

"Is he...?"

"You hear stuff," she shrugged.

"About him?"

"About him."

"Such as...?"

He knew better than to trust gossip, and college gossip was probably about as far from a reliable source as you could possibly get. But stories had to start somewhere...

"Like he has dated students in the past, a few years ago. Which is... just eeww. So I kinda hear you maybe don't want to get too close to him."

"Anyone currently?"

"Dunno."

"Okay. Thanks."

A student rushing somewhere bumped into him. Clumsy. Kid must play hockey, Lennox thought, knocked slightly off balance.

"Sorry, professor," the kid said, pausing for an instant.

He wore a denim jacket, and a knit cap with earflaps, down. Lennox blinked and it took just a second to remember that the last time he had seen this face, the kid had been wearing a top hat and swirling black cape, on the sidewalk outside the Musgrave mansion. The walking tour guide.

Dr. John Musgrave in the 1890s. The Biblical scholar. The Murderer's Bible...

"Sorry," the kid said again, not recognizing him. He hurried on his way across the quad and was gone.

"Hey there you two!"

Ellen.

Dammit.

And where was Prescott, anyway?

Despite the plastered-on smile, Lennox had to admit she looked great. New haircut, new glasses, new coat, unbuttoned to reveal that she had lost a few pounds. He'd always noticed that people tended to look either better or worse after a divorce, and she looked better, which made him think he must look worse. But he could still see his Ellen—the Ellen he'd fallen in love with, married, had a daughter with. The shy smart one.

"You're looking well, Drew," she smiled.

She'd called him Drew since their first date; Andrew had been her father's name, so that was too weird, she'd said, and she thought Andy just sounded silly.

"Not compared to you."

"Allie says you're on a case?"

He nodded. She probably thought he was there to plant drugs on Frazier and arrest him.

"That man they found out at Gallows Hill? I saw it in the news. It's awful. Are you making much progress?"

"Can't really go into it."

"Right, of course," she said awkwardly. "How's Ouellette?"

There was an edge in her voice as she asked. Ellen had always seemed jealous of Michelle Ouellette, the attractive woman her husband spent so much time with, worked so closely with. Who had that ass on her. Lennox wondered if this was some weird side-effect of a guilty conscience; if she was having an affair, he must be, too. Perhaps Ellen also wondered exactly who little Roland's father was.

"She's fine. She's fine."

He wasn't sure what else he could say.

And where the hell was Prescott? It was 1:20 now.

"I... I always liked you in that cap, Drew," Ellen said quietly, with a tiny shy smile. The same tiny shy smile that had first gotten his attention all those years ago.

"Thanks."

"Are you Detective Lennox? I'm Peter Prescott. I'm so sorry I'm late—I got caught up in something and couldn't get away."

Professor Peter Prescott was a big man with bushy hair and dark eyes, a few years older than Lennox, slightly winded from rushing over to the library to make their meeting. Jeans, silk shirt, the obligatory tweed jacket, and a book tucked under one arm. Blandly good looking, and Lennox quickly decided he might have even seemed glamorous to a starry-eyed girl from the Point.

"So you know Professor Faber?" Prescott asked, nodding toward Ellen.

Faber? She'd gone back to her maiden name? Of course she had.

"Yes, I know Professor Faber. This is our daughter, Allison."

"Your daughter—?" Prescott said slowly, looking from one face to another as it sank in.

Awkward greetings. Lennox wondered if he had enough Xanax for everyone.

"So, is there someplace we can talk?" Lennox asked.

"Yes, my office is this way…" Prescott took two steps away.

"Okay, so it was really good running into you both," Lennox stammered. "Ellen, you… you look great. And Allison, I'll talk to you in a couple days."

"I'll text you. Bye, Dad."

"Take care of yourself, Drew."

Lennox walked off with Prescott while his wife and daughter went in the opposite direction.

God, did he need a cigarette.

Prescott was right—Lennox never would have found his office. The professor led him up stairs and down halls and through several buildings—shortcuts, he explained—before finally opening the door to a cramped, book-lined office and switching on the light.

"You didn't say what you wanted to see me about when you called, Detective."

Of course not, Lennox thought. *If I had, you never would have agreed to meet with me.*

"I'm here about Annalisa Paiva."

Prescott froze.

"What about her?" he asked, picking at imaginary lint on his jacket.

"I've been assigned to reassess the case, and your name came up. The investigating officer spoke to you back then, didn't he?"

"Yes… a Detective Curwen, as I recall. We only met once. I had nothing to do with Annalisa's death. He understood that."

"You were sleeping with her, though."

Prescott made a little choking noise in the back of his throat. He slowly lowered himself into a chair and ran a hand through his hair.

"Yes, I was," he said slowly. "It was entirely consensual. I assure you. She was eighteen."

The part of Lennox that was a nine-year police veteran didn't care. The part of him that was the father of an eighteen year old daughter wanted a cigarette. Or to knock the man right out of his chair.

"Fine," he said. "Disgusting, but fine. I can't really care if you're sleeping with your students. But I do have to care when one of them gets killed."

"I had nothing to do with that."

"You're married, aren't you?"

"My wife is very understanding. And very… generous."

"Oh, I bet she is. So she knew about you and Annalisa?"

"Unfortunately, our relationship became the topic of some campus gossip. A number of people knew—a small number, including my wife."

"Bragging about your conquests, eh?"

"I don't like your tone, Detective."

And I don't like you despoiling people's daughters, Lennox thought.

"And no, I was perfectly discreet. Annalisa was the one who… bragged about her conquest, as you so crudely put it. But all of this is of course completely irrelevant. I had nothing to do with her death. The night Annalisa died, I was here on campus at a concert. I'm the faculty advisor for the chamber music club, and we had a Bach concert that night. I made a few introductory remarks, and then sat in the front row. The newspapers said she was killed between eight and nine o'clock, and I was here that entire time, with a roomful of people to vouch for me."

"Including your understanding, generous wife?"

"Actually, no. She was home with an awful migraine that night. It was a bad one—she was out of sorts for days after. Which is unfortunate. She loves Bach."

Lennox blinked, and then realized he was smiling.

"I'm sorry—she what now?"

Chapter XX

THE NEXT MORNING DWORACZYK GATHERED the detectives in the Major Case Room for a briefing. Lennox was the only one missing; no one had seen him since yesterday. Dworaczyk banged his hand on a metal desktop, calling, "Okay everybody, listen up. Michelle."

He nodded over to the uncomfortable Ouellette, standing by the whiteboard hung with crime scene photos and notes.

"Our primary goal right now is to place Charles Musgrave, also known as Paul Mather, in the Musgrave mansion anytime between Thursday, October 20, when he arrived in town, and Monday, October 24, when his body was found at Gallows Hill. They deny ever having any contact with him, but his cell phone records indicate that he called the family twice and spoke with them at some length. We can assume he visited the family home, but we still lack hard physical evidence, or a credible witness.

"I want to go back to the beginning and double-check everything. I'm going to assign several of you to re-canvass the neighborhood around Gallows Hill Park and the Musgrave house, working with uniformed officers. You'll start this after-noon."

"Trick or treat," a detective in back groaned.

"There better be candy..."

"And what are *you* supposed to be?" another laughed.

"Guys, settle down," Dworaczyk said sharply. "Sorry, Michelle, go on."

"This is the strangest family in town, and people notice them," she said. "Someone must have seen something that weekend. Lt. Winters has also signed off on offering a reward for information leading to the arrest and conviction of the guilty party or parties. Flyers with the information are being printed up now, and you'll distribute them as you canvass. Those of you assigned to the Musgrave neighborhood, I want flyers left on every car along that street, and leave two in their mailbox. I want them to know they're still under suspicion."

"How much is the reward?"

"Five thousand dollars."

"Taxes just went up!"

"I'm also having Johnson go over the family Bible again on the very slim chance that she missed something the first time. I know she didn't, but I'm having her check. On Monday, after Halloween, I'm starting up surveillance on the family again. Any questions so far? Good. So, I want—Mr. Mayor. Good morning."

Tobias Pyncheon swaggered into the bullpen, nodding and smiling, wearing a black suit with an orange tie. Of course. No doubt an expensively foreign black car was taking up two spaces outside. Two aides, one male, one female, both wearing mirror-shades, hung back, cellphones pressed to ears. Pyncheon probably liked to pretend they were Secret Service. The man quietly asked Winters to step back and give the Mayor room.

"Good morning, everyone. I just wanted to stop by and check in with you, and get a quick update on the murder investigation."

"We were just going over that. "

"Good. I also want to announce that I am personally adding another five thousand dollars to the reward money," he said with a self-satisfied smile. "People don't get killed in Salem; I want the perpetrator found."

"We will burn him at the stake when we do," Dworaczyk said. "Just like the old days."

"It's already pretty busy out there," the Mayor went on, "and I don't need to tell you that every year I'm very, very proud of the job this department does in keeping the streets safe and the tourists happy. I know it'll be a strain this year with this investigation going on, and I want to thank you men—and of course you, Sergeant Ouellette, is it?—for all your hard work in advance. Good luck to you all tonight."

He glanced at his Rolex, spun, and left the bullpen, off to make his next speech at his next appearance. The Mayor of Salem probably had fifty stops to make on Halloween, most no longer than the two minutes he'd just spent in the bullpen. Unless there were television cameras. And he still had to leave time to get home to hand out full-size candy bars to trick-or-treaters.

"So will Gilman kick in another five thousand now?" someone asked as Pyncheon vanished down the hall.

"He'll kick in six," someone else chortled.

"That'll be all for now, unless anyone has anything to add? Nothing? Okay, thank you. Remember, Sergeant Dworaczyk and I will be based here tonight." Ouellette said. "And check the call sheet for your overnight assignments."

"See, this is the way it should be, Michelle," Dworaczyk said, taking a seat next to her desk as the detectives dispersed. "Real policework. You need a real cop for a partner, not Lennox. I mean no offense, but the guy is a weirdo. I do not know how you put up with him sometimes, I swear."

She turned to her laptop and tried to ignore him.

"Look, Halloween is going to be mental around here, always is, especially on a Saturday night. When we get off shift tomorrow, I know a great little breakfast place over on Rockport we can grab a bite. Place serves a great bloody Mary. Something to think about, Michelle."

"Work to do," she said quietly.

"Well, you just keep it in mind."

"They didn't burn witches at the stake here," she said. "They hanged them."

"Yeah, well…" he shrugged. "Whatever."

Ouellette looked over to the empty desk across from her.

Lennox would have known better.

The Prescott house was in Marblehead, and was much nicer than Lennox would have thought a state university professor could afford. Done in turn-of the-century brick, the two-story house with a garden and garage sat comfortably relaxed in the middle of a nice neighborhood, and Marblehead seemed to consist of nothing but nice neighborhoods. A big pale jack-o-lantern grimaced at him from the front steps.

Louisa Prescott answered his knock and looked quizzically at him in the early morning sunshine. He showed his gold badge and introduced himself as a detective from the Salem PD.

"What's this about?" she asked.

She was similar to her husband, both well-dressed WASPs who evidently looked after themselves in various ways. Louisa seemed like someone who had a martini when she got back from Pilates.

"I'm going back over the death of Annalisa Paiva," Lennox said. "I need to ask you a couple of questions."

"I don't see what that has to do with me," she said, her voice catching slightly on her words.

"It should only take a few minutes, we just need to clear up a couple of things on an old case. So let me see here…"

He opened his organizer and scowled as checked the various pockets and flaps.

"Oh, come on," he muttered. "I had it before. I'm sorry, ma'am, I apparently left the file back at the station, and it has my notes in it, and all the stuff I was going to ask about. Could… could I just run you over there for a couple of minutes? I've been having a really crazy week, believe me. This would be a huge help…"

He shrugged and smiled.

Here I am, he thought. *The harmless, bumbling cop, the Barney Fife who can't even remember to bring his notes with him. Here I am,* he thought, *the detective investigating a six-year-old homicide, who wants to bring you back into his jurisdiction, put you in an interrogation room, and close this damn case.*

"I can have you down there and back in no time. You'll be back in time for trick-or-treaters, and I *know* you're looking forward to that."

He gave a little chuckle. So did she. A start.

"I can even promise you a cup of our famous station house coffee. It's the worst in town. You have my guarantee."

Louisa sighed and gave in. She got a jacket and locked the door behind her as they went out, leaves crunching underfoot.

The fluorescent lights in Interview Room Two showed how worried Louisa Prescott was as she took a seat in a hard plastic chair. She now looked much older than she had out in the sunlight. Lennox's demeanor had changed as they entered the station, his mouth becoming a firm line as he held the door for her and guided her into the small room with the harsh lighting. The same room Benedict Musgrave had occupied two days ago.

He beckoned those spectral girls and phantom judges close. A Devil's bargain, he knew, but he needed them now.

"I really don't know what I can tell you," she stammered.

Lennox tore the end off an evidence envelope and poured the contents out. Six leather coat buttons bounced and skittered on the tabletop.

"What—what are those?" she asked.

"You know what they are," he replied.

Louisa blanched and curled in on herself, hunched, hands between her knees. Not looking at the buttons on the table. Not looking at them very, very hard.

"I don't."

She looked and him, then looked away, unsure where to put her eyes.

"Your husband had Annalisa Paiva in one of his classes," he began without even glancing at the yellow legal pad of notes on the table in front of him. "Which class was that?"

"Western Civ," she said quietly. "It's a requirement. He... he hates teaching it."

"And when did you first meet her?"

"I don't remember."

"Yes, you do. You remember exactly when you met her, and you knew exactly what was going on the minute you saw her. The minute you saw *them*."

"I have no idea what you mean."

"He was sleeping with her, and you knew it the minute you saw her. When was that?"

When she didn't answer, he moved the buttons across the table one by one, like checkers. Clacking them down hard.

"Christmas party," she murmured. "Department Christmas party. Faculty and students were there. She was there. He'd had too much to drink. It was... obvious. He was just obvious."

"There had been others."

"Yes... but he'd kept quiet about it," she whispered.

"So that was it."

"That was what?"

"Word got out. You were angry about it. Angry at her, or him?"

"*Both.*"

The word came up from somewhere deep and dark.

"I was—I guess. It had always been kept quiet before. I didn't... care... as long as no one found out."

"Different this time, though, right? Different than the other times. Different because...?"

"Stupid little slut couldn't keep her mouth shut, had to go tell her girlfriends. *Bitch.*"

"So people were talking and he expected you to just stand there while everyone knew he was screwing around with *another* one of his students."

"Made me a laughingstock."

"I'd want to give her a piece of my mind, too, tell her to stay the hell away—"

"I didn't care about that—she could have him, for all I cared. I have someone else, too. Just keep your damn stupid mouth shut about it."

"So you confronted her."

Louisa's head snapped up. She seemed to come out of whatever trance she had slipped into a moment before, and Lennox thought he might have lost his chance with her, like he had with Laura the day before.

"You've been carrying this around for a long time now. Six years is a hell of a long time. You haven't been able to talk to anyone about this for years. And it's been weighing you down, hasn't it, Louisa?"

She nodded slowly. She was teetering. She just needed the gentlest nudge…

You could only keep secrets for so long. Eventually, he knew, the balance tipped and the secrets kept you.

"I know what it's like to have something you can't tell anyone about, believe me. Let me help you. Let me take that weight off your shoulders, Louisa."

She had reached that point. Everyone did, eventually.

"I… went to see her."

"And what happened?"

"Tuesday nights, she had class. She took a bus from campus to downtown and walked a few blocks home. I… I found this out by following her."

"So one Tuesday night you followed her, and you confronted her."

"He was going to his damn concert, so I told him I was going to stay home. Said I had a headache. I knew he'd be gone for hours. Once he was gone I drove over to Ward Street and waited. And eventually she came walking down the street. She put her key in the door of her building, and I got out of the car. I started… yelling at her, and she backed up. She kept looking around like she was afraid someone was going to hear us. She went back around the corner of the building and… she looked so scared of me. My God, she was just a scared girl."

She reached over and gingerly picked up one button, staring at it. Lennox wondered just what she was seeing there as she ran one finger along the raised design.

"Then what happened, Louisa?"

"I grabbed her by the arm and she pulled away from me, she said something, something in Portuguese. I grabbed her again by the front of her coat and she pulled back… the buttons… the buttons went everywhere. She slapped me and… and I pushed her. I pushed her and she fell over backwards and went right down those steps."

"And then?"

"And then she didn't move. I ran like hell."

"Did you tell Peter?"

"No," she said in a dry whisper. "I never told anyone, until now."

"Louisa, I'm placing you under arrest for the murder of Annalisa Paiva. Do you understand?"

"God, she was just a kid…"

She fell forward on the table and covered her head with her hands.

"Well done, detective," Winters said an hour later, shaking his hand. Genuinely pleased. "Very nice indeed."

"She'll probably get manslaughter," Lennox said thoughtfully. "There was malice, but no real criminal intent. She didn't mean to kill that girl."

"That's for the lawyers. For us, we have closed the case. You have a closed case, detective."

"Yeah," he said. "How are Ouellette and Dworaczyk doing on the Musgrave case?"

"They're following leads," Winters nodded, obviously not wanting to go into it. "Working the case. But it's not something you need to worry about just now."

"I'm ready to get back to it."

"We can talk about that later, Andrew. Take the night off. Don't tell anyone."

"Thank you, sir. I have a few stops to make first."

Halloween in Salem. A Saturday this year. And a full moon.

And it was a beautiful night. Clear dark skies, bright stars, a breeze warm one moment, chill the next in that fickle perfect Autumn way. The bare branches of trees spread out against the night and swayed in the wind, ancient and aloof. Winter was coming, with frost and cold and blankets of white. But tonight, Autumn held court.

It took Lennox over an hour to get home from the station. The streets were choked with sheeted ghosts and pirates and medieval wenches walking almost blindly out in front of his car, too drunk or too excited to care. Cowboys, evil clowns, and hockey-masked killers walked arm in arm, shoulder to shoulder with gladiators, mad scientists, and vampires. College girls cackled and waved handcuffs and nearly spilled out of tiny police costumes. Zombies staggered by, women flashed strangers who tossed candy back to them, and red-faced devils brandished pitchforks, shrieking *"Happy Halloween motherfuckahs!"*

Most of them had no idea exactly where they were, or what they were doing, they just knew they were somewhere in Salem, and it was Halloween, and tomorrow was forever away.

A hundred kinds of music echoed from every corner, competing with fireworks, vuvuzelas, and the babble of countless tongues. Fried dough and kettle corn and balloons rode the changing breeze. A Ferris wheel cast long, weird shadows over a Colonial graveyard.

A man with a bullhorn stood on a folding chair, exhorting people to turn their lives over to the Lord, for God so loved the world he gave his one and only Son, that whoever believes in him shall not perish but have eternal life. Witches in robes tried to drown him out with air horns.

Hundreds of police officers were on loan from other cities throughout the Commonwealth. Cruisers prowled down the crowded streets, blue and red lights strobing and flashing. Foot patrols worked their way through the crush of people, along with cops on bikes and even segways. Mounted patrol cleared a path as they trotted along, the throngs parting around them.

He was tired and hungry, inching along in traffic, weary in his bones, but he smiled. Under all the noise and the crowds and the crass, there was real magic to this night, a pulsing, joyous, vital magic. Older than the world. All those revelers were somehow right—tomorrow *didn't* matter. Tonight was Halloween, with its special one-night-only alchemy. Put on a mask, be someone else or finally be exactly who you had secretly been all along. Bark at the moon. Fall in love. Remember. Or forget for a while. The Great Wheel of the year was turning, and tomorrow was a blank slate. But even then, you'd still have tonight. And the very thought made him smile.

Halloween in Salem. A Saturday this year. And a full moon.

He finally reached the old jail, and slowly made his way up the stairs. Neighbors' kids in store-bought costumes stalked the halls. Trick or treat. Most parents would probably restrict their kids to apartment complexes this year, or quieter suburban streets, rather than risk the licentious madness downtown. Most of the kids were still too young for a Salem Halloween anyway, he thought.

He locked his door, turned off the lights, and ignored the doorbell, pretending not to be home.

Closing a case usually resulted in a thrill of satisfaction, even elation. The sense of catching a bad guy, bringing the guilty to account, getting justice for the victim—these things usually stayed with him for days, keeping him warm and worthy. And closing the Paiva case was gratifying, no matter how much sympathy he may have ended up feeling for Louisa Prescott. The nods and thankful tears of the Paiva family gave him some taste of the usual warmth, as did the stoic, grateful handshake from Antonio. But all that was quickly replaced by the hard knowledge that he was now the only detective in the CID without a case, the only one *not* working the murder of Charles Musgrave.

And Laura might never wake up.

He wanted a cigarette. The square silver case with his initials still sat on the coffee table, mocking and empty.

He went into the bathroom, opening the medicine cabinet, reaching for the nondescript white box the blister packs of Xanax came in.

Empty.

Dammit. He hadn't been hitting them that hard. He thought. But then he hadn't been home that much lately either, so it was possible he had lost track. The empty box only turned up the heat on the anxiety that had been simmering in him all day.

He checked the pockets of the L. L. Bean coat tossed over the back of a chair by the door.

Also empty.

He switched on the coffee maker on the kitchen counter and then sat, wishing he had a television, wishing he could numbly channel surf for a couple of hours until falling asleep on the couch. It was past eleven o'clock. On another night, a better night, sleep might still be far away, but tonight he would be damn lucky if it came at all. The coffee maker hissed and gurgled as he thought of the Xanax tablets in his right hand drawer at the station. He knew he still had at least a dozen there.

Do I really want to drive over there to get my pills? he wondered. Doesn't that make me some kind of addict?

Still, if he did go by the station, he could spend a few minutes going over the final report on the Paiva case. He'd be submitting it Monday morning, and giving it one last read-through wasn't a bad idea, was it?

He turned off the coffee maker. He'd walk. Quicker that way.

Chapter XXI

THE DESK SERGEANT BUZZED HIM IN and he made his way upstairs.

On any other night of the year, the station would be quiet as midnight approached, the only excitement being a routine shift change. But October was different, and Halloween was completely different. Salem officers stood in the bright corridors, drinking coffee and laughing or commiserating with out-of-town police, swapping stories back and forth. Radios crackled and mixed with laughter and shouts ringing off the walls. The flow of uniforms never stopped, in and out like a blue tide. Scanners chattered and whispered and somewhere down the hallway, Johnny Cash sang about shooting a man in Reno just to watch him die. A pile of confiscated weapons rose behind the duty desk, swords and knives and axes and guns; only some of them were fake. The holding cells were nearly full with drunk-and-disorderlies, pickpockets, and a couple of assaults.

A busy night. As expected.

He went up to Halloween Central. On the last night of October, the upstairs conference room was turned into the department's command center, with banks of monitors along one entire wall, hooked to security camera all across downtown. Homeland Security money was well spent in Salem on Halloween. Dozens of officers crammed into the room, hunched over laptops, whispering into cell phones, staring at the rows of monitors. The atmosphere here was completely different from downstairs—no laughter, no banter. Everyone was tensed, on high alert, watching and waiting for situations that needed to be clamped down upon before they got out of control. For many people, Halloween was the best night of the year in Salem, but for cops, it was easily the worst.

No one noticed Lennox as he came in, glanced around the room for Ouellette, and slipped back out when he didn't see her.

Ouellette looked up as he came into the bullpen a moment later, giving him a tired smile. Her cufflinks tonight were tiny glass jack-o-lanterns. She had a sense of humor, Lennox knew, but sometimes he had to squint to see it. There were two pencils stuck in her ponytail, and her desk was a pile of paper.

"Congratulations on closing Paiva," she said.

"Thanks," he said, taking his seat across from her. "Where's Dworaczyk?"

"He's out on a call. How is it out there?"

"Crazy. Any estimates?"

"Thirty, forty thousand," she said. Thirty or forty thousand partygoers descending on a city of forty thousand residents was no joke. "That's what I've been hearing."

He opened the right hand drawer of his desk, popped a pill through the foil backing and washed it down with a five-dollar bottle of water he'd bought from a street vendor on the way over. It left a chalky bitterness as it went down. He didn't care anymore if she saw. He was too tired.

"Antianxiety meds," Ouellette said. "Valium, something like that?"

"Xanax," he blinked. "How'd you know?"

"You weren't very good at hiding it."

He nodded.

"That raid gave you a good scare."

"Never shot anyone," he said, letting out a slow breath. "Never had to. But… when I turned around and he had that gun…"

"You defended yourself," she said. "I would have done the same. Any one of us would have. The inquiry cleared you, the AG didn't pursue it. You know you did the right thing, Andrew."

Pause.

"But… that the report you filed doesn't tell the whole story, does it?"

"No, it does not."

"So, what happened up there?"

He hesitated. Charles Musgrave had been killed to keep the family secret from getting out; Annalisa Paiva had been killed *because* a secret had gotten out. Secrets were things with sharp edges, things to be handled carefully. He had to tell her, he realized only now. Because the secret had been keeping him.

The events leading up to the raid had started months before, with a noticeable spike in drug traffic and related crimes. For reasons unknown and widely speculated upon, Salem had always lagged a decade or more behind other cities when it came to the drug trade. Methamphetamine gangs might be devouring other cities, but had never caught on in Salem, where cocaine and heroin still cornered the local drug market. But over the summer, word was that a new gang had moved in, a hungry, brutal, organized operation that either ran the competition out or brought them aboard. The drug of choice became crack, and soon empty vials and shattered pipes littered the gutters of the Point.

Dworaczyk had been assigned to handle a series of low-level arrests, hoping to slowly work his way up the food chain to the bosses. It took weeks of buy-busts, but eventually he had a list of names and an address; the dealers operated out of a crumbling piece of subsidized housing on a narrow back street. He obtained a warrant and assembled the other CID officers and a dozen uniforms for what many rightfully saw as a career-making case. Dealers-turned-informant, hoping for lighter sentences, warned them that the gang was well-armed, so Kevlar vests and extra clips were distributed. Serious business.

"I was right behind Dworaczyk when he went through the door with the first wave of uniforms," Lennox began, wondering if he'd need another Xanax to get through the story. "I went through the kitchen to that back bedroom. There was an officer right behind me… Foley. Dealers were running everywhere—I heard Dworaczyk say later that there were twice as many guys there as he'd been expecting. It was just crazy."

"I was there," Ouellette said quietly. "I remember."

It had been chaos. Twenty police officers, detectives and uniforms, burst into the dingy apartment building, brandishing rifles and warrants. Dealers scrambled madly. Two of them actually jumped out third-story windows. Those who didn't escape were rounded up and confined to one room, wrists and ankles bound with zip-ties.

"There was a scuffle, and Foley steps out of the bedroom to help deal with it. And I open this little closet door, with my gun ready, to make sure it's clear."

"Which is a stupid thing to do if you're alone like that."

"So I open the closet door," he went on, ignoring her. "And… there's Katherine Bowen."

"Who?"

"We were in the Coast Guard together, back on my first tour. She was a good kid, but you could tell it was all kind of an effort for her. She had a temper, and that didn't help. One time…" he chuckled at the memory coming back. "One time, we stopped this big yacht to do a safety check. We'd do a couple of these a day. You go aboard, make sure their pumps are working, make sure their flares are less than a year old, make sure they have life jackets for everyone on board… basic stuff. Takes about fifteen minutes, we'd hand them a certificate and send them on their way. Just routine.

"So we stopped this huge yacht one time, and really, we stopped it just because we wanted to go aboard and have a look around. It was beautiful. Well, we go aboard, and the owner is completely drunk; he has his son piloting the vessel. He does not want the Coast Guard coming onto his two-million-dollar yacht and checking things out. So I turn to go below-decks and make sure he isn't taking on water… and he shoves me down the stairs."

"You're kidding?" Ouellette said.

"I am not. It's only a few steps, but still, it's kind of like assaulting an officer. I pick myself up and turn around… and Kathy has the guy in a half-nelson and she's bent him over the railing." He laughed as the image came back to him. "Any further and he'd have gone over. She got written up all to hell and back for that. That's kind of who she was—she was a hothead, but she didn't take shit from anyone."

Lennox sighed and leaned back in his chair. "In her third year, she… she got thrown out."

"What did she do?" Ouellette asked. "Sink one of your boats?"

"No. Failed a drug test. That's all it takes in the service, one failed test and you're out. She went home—she'd mentioned that she was from Gloucester, from a long line of fishermen. After I started as a patrolman, I saw her a few times here in town, which surprised the hell out of me. Just a weird coincidence. And she always had some crappy job—liquor store cashier, graveyard shift at a convenience store, that sort of thing. And I knew she wasn't doing well.

"The last couple of times I saw her, I had just made detective, and I could tell she was using. She had the little burns on her fingers, you know? From holding the pipe?"

"And you just ignored it."

"And I just ignored it."

"So she was hiding in the closet," she said.

"Yeah, she was hiding in the closet. And we stared at each other, it seemed like forever, and neither of us said a damn thing. She wasn't part of the gang, she was there to buy. Why the hell she didn't buy out on a corner like everyone else is beyond me. When we all came in, she panicked, and crawled into the closet to hide. She was terrified."

Like poor Laura Musgrave, he thought. Laura, who might never wake up.

"And you know all of this because… you've spoken to her since?"

"Yes. So I open the closet, and there she is. And then that scuffle that Foley stepped out for gets out of hand. One of the dealers, Dontay Williams, knocks Foley down and gets his gun away from him."

"Dontay elbowed me about five minutes before this happened, by the way." Ouellette ran a finger along her jaw.

"So there's Dontay in the doorway of the back bedroom, with a gun. Foley's gun. And, because I am very, very well trained... Dontay took two to the chest before he could even get it pointed at me. I kicked the closet door closed behind me as he went down. I called clear, and Kathy must have stayed put and snuck out hours later when it was quiet."

"And her name appears nowhere in the report you filed on the shooting."

"Nowhere."

Ouellette shifted uncomfortably in her chair.

"She's a junkie, she's miserable, she has no one," Lennox said. "Arresting her does no one any good. Keeping her out of the report is the lesser evil here. I've made some calls trying to find her a bed in a rehab. She belongs in a hospital, not jail."

"You're probably right."

"Yeah, probably. I mean, what else could I do? I had to keep quiet. Keep it... secret."

A long silence in the bullpen.

"So, where are you on Musgrave?" he asked clumsily.

"Pretty much the same place we were," she replied. "Monday, we continue canvassing, I have Johnson going over the Bible again—"

"The Bible," Lennox blinked. "Dammit. The Bible. That's right. I was so wrapped up in Paiva I forgot."

"Forgot what?"

"I saw the tour guide again—the kid from outside the mansion."

"And?"

"Remember the spiel? Dr. John Musgrave in the 1890s. The Biblical scholar..."

"The one... the one who collected Bibles."

"The one who collected Bibles," he smiled.

"They gave us one of his Bibles."

"Yes. The family Bible—the one that Laura was trying to tell me about, the one with our evidence—is still somewhere in that house."

"*Merde.*"

They were interrupted by a call on the radio on Ouellette's desk.

"All units, all units, 10-57. Firearms discharged."

They both recognized the address given.

The Musgrave house.

"Speak of the devil."

Ouellette took her Glock and two extra clips from the locked drawer of her desk, and reached for her vest.

"You sure you're ready for this?" she asked.

"Yeah."

"Let's go. I'm driving."

Chapter XXII

THEY SPED ACROSS TOWN, the Crown Vic's lights and siren clearing a path through the crowds still thronging the streets. But Ouellette still needed to lean on the horn and shout over the vehicle's loudspeaker, *"Move!"* She cut down narrow side streets and through pedestrian areas in ways Lennox never would have dared. They arrived at the Musgrave mansion just behind the first cruiser, a Salem cruiser, and red and blue lights flickered and flashed across the mansion's stern façade.

The front door was half-open. Exiting the vehicle, Lennox saw the muddy smear of a bootprint just below the leering brass knocker, the splintered wood of the doorjamb.

Familiar, he thought, with his compact S&W .40 caliber cold and heavy in his hand. Too familiar, approaching an old brick building and knowing only dread. The Musgrave house was grander than anything in the Point, certainly, but its inhabitants, he'd come to learn over the past few weeks, were far more dangerous than any street thug or corner dealer to be found there. Hopefully, no one would end up dead tonight. But he knew that was only partly under his control.

A flash of movement as a man burst out the front door.

Ski mask, leather jacket, with a pistol in one hand, something small. A .22 maybe. His other hand held something to his chest—square, bulky. A large book.

The Musgrave family Bible.

Ouellette's gun came up.

"Police!" she shouted. *"Don't move... Merde!"*

193

The man scrambled, changed direction, and ran like hell into the night.

Benedict now came running out the door, pale and drawn and carrying a long iron poker from the fireplace. He didn't seem to even notice the police as he set off after the man carrying the ancient Bible.

Ouellette motioned the two uniforms toward the house as she and Lennox went after Benedict and the other man. The detectives dodged around a wave of cruisers arriving on scene as they ran.

Benedict and his quarry pelted down a narrow alley, with Lennox and Ouellette behind them.

Too far behind them, Lennox realized. He glanced back over his shoulder. Ouellette was right there, keeping pace with those long legs. A few more streets, a few more alleys, and they plunged into the tourists of Essex Street.

As midnight passed, the face of the crowd had changed. Masks were off, makeup smeared, costumes disheveled, the fun ebbing. Many, most, were tired or drunk or high. It was last call, last chance for Halloween in Salem, many wrapped up in their own private little worlds as everything revolved hazily around them.

Benedict shoved tourists out of his way, while ahead of him, the man with the Bible dodged and wove nimbly around them. A few drunks picked themselves up from the pavement, fists ready, but fell back when they realized the poker wasn't part of a costume.

The ski mask rode up the man's neck as he ran, revealing a spiky tribal tattoo across the side of his neck. Lennox remembered that tattoo.

Eric Scully, the man who tried to break into the Musgrave mansion. Out on bail and finishing what he'd set out to do a week ago. Scully must have recognized Ouellette, and he peeled off the ski mask and let it fall. In a crowd, a face stood out less than a ski mask.

Lennox's lungs started to burn, pains shooting up his legs. This was no pleasant little jog around the Common.

"Police!" he shouted. "Stop those men!"

But that only cleared a space for them, as tourists whirled, surprised, and stepped out of the way. Just as well, really—a bleary crowd like this was as likely to trip an officer as stop the suspect.

"Heading south on Essex—" he heard Ouellette rasp into her radio. Then she fell into a long string of French-Canadian invective as she ran.

They ran past Pendragon's, the corseted greeter watching them go. Past the cover band singing Monster Mash, past the fried dough vendor and the living statue. Past the Peabody-Essex Museum and past the visitors' center, both open until midnight. Scully darted across Hawthorne Boulevard and into the Common, with Benedict right behind.

Benedict had ten years on him, Lennox thought, but was in better shape than he appeared, keeping up with the fleeing man. But it was probably down to motivation.

Lennox saw a pair of uniforms coming up the Boulevard in answer to Ouellette's alert. He pointed them into the Common.

The crowded, roiling Common.

Halloween. The most important night in the witches' calendar. The biggest night in Salem. And the Common was Ground Zero.

And it was packed. Witches in robes and capes, with drums and candles, calling to the gods, the goddesses, the earth and the sky as tourists and news crews jostled one another for the best shot. Half a dozen card tables were scattered throughout the crowd—vendors hawking incense and crystals and *Hanging Around In Salem* t-shirts. The only clearing was a circle around a great bonfire lit to welcome the coming year. There must have been five hundred people here, Lennox thought. Or maybe twice that—no time to pay attention to anyone but the two men he was pursuing.

Magnus Moon stood atop a small platform of cinder blocks and two-by-fours draped in a purple cloth. He wore a sweeping velvet cloak, holding a long staff in one hand and a microphone in the other. For Magnus, it was part religion, part showbiz. Always. He lifted the heavy staff to the four directions and invoked the spirits of those who had crossed over in the past year.

"To all ye who gather here tonight, let us say this," Magnus intoned solemnly. "Those spirits are all somehow present and never far, on this night, of all nights! And this night, of all nights, we pause to remember the poor man who died alone and unknown and was left hanging at Gallows Hill, adding injustice to injustice!"

A ring of witches slowly circled the bonfire, brandishing brooms and wands. Their long cloaks swept the grass as they moved. The rest of the crowd—the tourists, the news reporters looking for colorful footage, and the gawkers—stood back behind sawhorses, keeping them at a distance. There were firetrucks on either side of the common, lights flashing, waiting.

Eric Scully broke the circle, vaulting over the platform and knocking down Magnus as he went.

Benedict was right behind him. As Magnus struggled to his feet, Benedict wound up and hurled the iron poker. It flew end over end with a whisper, striking Scully in the back of his head wetly. He pitched forward, landing face down on the ground. Not moving.

The assembled witches recoiled together, gasping and stumbling back, shocked that their holiest of nights should be interrupted, should be blasphemed.

When Scully hit the ground, the old Bible flew from his grasp and tumbled away a few feet. His pistol slid off in the opposite direction.

Benedict, his breath coming in ragged gasps, fell to his knees next to the Bible. He picked up the ancient book with both hands and held it over his head.

All the proof you need is in the family Bible...

Harker had answered a domestic disturbance call right after the detectives' initial interview of the family. Laura said she thought Benedict was going to hit their mother. What had they disagreed about so fiercely?

The Bible, Lennox now realized, as Benedict pulled himself to his feet. The Bible and whatever evidence it contained. Benedict wanted to destroy it, keeping it out of the hands of the police forever, and Agatha, twisted old matriarch of a twisted old family, wouldn't allow it. They'd argued. Viciously. Almost violently. Benedict went to a tarot reader for advice, but whatever Symboline Carto had told him, Agatha had the last word. The Bible would not be destroyed.

But Agatha wasn't here.

Benedict whirled and heaved the Bible into the fire.

Ouellette launched herself, arms wide, reaching for the book as it tumbled toward the flames.

It slipped through her hands as she grasped at it, her fingers closing around air.

Sparks flew as the Bible landed in the bonfire, embers tumbled and spilled onto the ground.

She hit the ground hard but fell loose, her years with Mounted having taught her how to take a fall.

"*We cannot allow you—*" Magnus Moon shouted.

Back on her feet, Ouellette spun and took the long staff from him, his long wizard's staff studded with crystals and ringed with iron bands. She plunged one end into the fire, under the Bible, and flipped the smoldering old book up and out of the flames. Benedict scrambled for it when it landed.

But Ouellette had dropped the staff and now pointed her Glock at him.

"*Don't,*" was all she said.

Benedict collapsed back onto the grass and wept raggedly.

Lennox looked over to where Scully's gun lay—at someone's feet. Someone neither cloaked nor costumed, someone who now reached down, picked the gun up, and pointed it back at him.

Christopher Maitland.

Maitland?

What the hell was he doing here?

Maitland's eyes went to Scully splayed out a few yards away.

Then Lennox realized, despite how hard his head spun, that Maitland had sent Scully to steal the Bible. Whatever proof was in there implicated him as well as the Musgraves. It must.

Why else would he want it? And the Common on Halloween was the perfect place for a handoff—only too easy to get lost in that crowd.

Now there was uncertainty in Maitland's eyes. He'd probably picked up the gun before he even quite realized what he was doing. And now—now he raised the gun up in the air, up over his head, and fired. The gunshot echoed across the Common as the crowd panicked.

Those on the fringes of the circle bolted, screaming. Those closer to the center, around the bonfire, who had gotten there early or had pushed their way through the throng for a better view, hit the ground. Heads in hands, arms wrapped around others, some couldn't look while others couldn't look away.

The plan was ruined now. No chance of a quiet handoff, with Maitland and Scully melting away anonymously into the crowd. He didn't have a plan now, he only had a gun, and he leveled it at Lennox.

And Lennox was looking down a barrel. Again. He swung his gun up. He couldn't breathe.

The only sound to be heard was the crackle of the bonfire.

The ghost of Dontay Williams whispered *"Bang!"* in his ear. How many times had he replayed those fatal few seconds in his mind? Foley. The scuffle. The gun. Dontay. The loudest sound he'd ever heard. How many sleepless nights? How many therapy sessions? How many pills? Too many. Too much doubt, too much second guessing, too much wondering and not nearly enough knowing. Trying to choose Life over Death and not sure that he could.

There were a hundred people in every direction, and in the middle of them an uncertain man with a gun, Christopher Maitland. An armed suspect, innocent bystanders, civilians in harm's way—Lennox had to shoot him, no question.

But if his hand shook, if a stiff breeze nudged the bullet even slightly—there were a hundred people in every direction. Innocent bystanders. Civilians in harm's way.

And if Maitland shot first…

A figure stepped out of the crowd—one of the witches, in a long cloak of blood red velvet, the hood up, face in shadow. A hand came from the folds of the cloak, a hand with a pistol, pressing the gun to Christopher Maitland's temple.

A Smith and Wesson .40 caliber—the standard-issue service weapon on the Salem PD.

Shaking the hood down with a snap of her head, Elizabeth Harker's long blonde hair spilled over her shoulders. She didn't take her eyes from Maitland, her jaw tight and her mouth grim.

"Salem PD," she said. "Drop it."

The pistol landed silently in the grass at his feet.

"You are just all the hell under arrest," Lennox rasped, holstering his own weapon and doubling over, hands on knees, blood singing in his ears as he tried to catch his breath. He knew that as soon as the adrenaline stopped racing through him, he'd probably be sprawled out on the grass next to Benedict and Scully. He looked over to Harker. "How did you get tonight off?"

"I'm supposed to be on light duty," she said. "Anyone have cuffs?"

Lennox staggered over to Ouellette on rubber legs. She had rolled Benedict over and cuffed him. As he helped her to her feet, she seemed to notice something amiss, and turned to scan the ground.

"*Merde*," she murmured.

"What?"

"When I hit the ground… I think I lost a cufflink. They don't make this style anymore."

Lennox laughed and spent a moment looking from Benedict, to Maitland, to the prone figure of Scully, and finally to the Bible. And things began to click over in his mind as he did so.

Magnus pushed his way through the crowd, pressing through the circle closing around the police. He paused to lay a hand upon his breast.

"We saw it all, constable…" he intoned.

"I'll get a statement later," Lennox said over his shoulder. Much later. With help from the uniforms, he and Ouellette and Harker gathered up their suspects and the Bible, and headed back to the Musgrave mansion. The crowd applauded and parted before them as they made their way to the gate on Hawthorne Boulevard.

Chapter XXIII

IT WAS ALMOST TWO IN THE MORNING when they arrived back at the mansion—Lennox, Ouellette, Harker, and handful of uniforms with Benedict, Maitland, and the Bible-stealing Scully in tow.

News crews followed them from the Common. As the strange little parade of police and suspects made their way across town, reporters jogged alongside, thrusting microphones and cameras at them, asking for statements. Lennox said "No comment" about every third step. When they reached the Musgrave mansion, news vans were already waiting. The detectives carefully guided the suspects over cables and around camera equipment to the front door.

Maitland entered the house reluctantly, literally dragging his feet. With the hand gripping his arm, Lennox felt the man shudder as they moved down the hall and into the parlor.

Agatha, in her wheelchair by the fire, locked eyes with Maitland as they entered.

With a shriek, she threw off the plaid blanket tucked around her knees and lurched across the room to where Maitland stood, frozen in place. She raised her gnarled hands with their ragged, parchment-colored nails and went for him. He raised one arm but was rooted to the spot, unable to step out of the way as she came for him. She would have clawed his eyes out if Ouellette hadn't been so quick, hooking an arm around the old woman's waist and forcing her over to the table and into a chair.

Agatha crumpled into the chair, suddenly looking very old and frail and pathetic. She knew it was over, that control of the situation had long since slipped her grasp. The fall of the house of Musgrave. Lennox could see the resignation in her tired face—the same resignation he had seen in Louisa Prescott.

Had that really only been this afternoon? he wondered. It felt like forever ago.

The old woman fumbled silently with her pipe, filling the bowl with the foul tobacco and packing it down with her thumb. Her hands shook and she clenched her teeth and a moment later the pipe dropped from her fingers and tobacco scattered across the tabletop.

"Dammit," she hissed. "God damn it."

She started to sob then, deep dry sobs that wracked her thin frame.

Stepping away, Lennox surveyed the room. The portrait of Silas Musgrave scowled down from high over the mantelpiece. It took Lennox a moment to realize that Silas's eyes, once so flinty and disdainful, had been shot out. Now they were just holes, as empty as Silas's soul. Firearm discharged, indeed.

Opposite the yawning fireplace was the massive floor-to-ceiling bookcase he had caught himself admiring when he and Ouellette first interviewed the family. The bookcase now angled away from the wall, and Lennox realized that it was a door. Behind it was a low archway and... stairs. Ageless, rough-hewn steps, spotted with moss and damp. Stairs leading down.

Part of the original house, part of Silas's house, the hidden cellars that had escaped God's fiery judgment upon the old reprobate. The secret chambers where he despoiled local virgins two or three at a time and practiced his unspeakable black arts. Benedict's old girlfriend had been right—there were tunnels beneath Musgrave buildings but it had been the mansion, not the mill. Another half-remembered story, not quite right. Typical Salem.

He borrowed a big Maglite from one of the uniforms and its beam played down the steps and along the crumbling brick walls.

"Five minutes," he called to Ouellette over his shoulder.

"No," she said. "We have work to do here."

"Exigent circumstances."

"No," she replied firmly.

"Fine."

He snapped off the flashlight and turned his attention to the old family Bible now resting on the great table in the center of the room. It was weathered and worn with the passage of three centuries and countless hands upon it. It was singed from the bonfire, still smelling faintly of smoke, with fresh mud smeared along the spine.

Lennox was not a religious man. Being shuttled from one Army base to another growing up, there had just never been time. Even in his adult life, he had simply never bothered to seek out a church; he and Ellen had been married by a Justice of the Peace. But despite his lack of any religion and his tendency to leave the question of God open, he approached this particular Bible with a kind of reverence—not only because of its age and its history, but because it was the missing piece. The final nail in the Musgrave coffin.

He gently opened the big book, gingerly turning pages, and he and Ouellette saw what was inside. They finally had the whole story.

"You realize that we've gathered all the suspects in the parlor, don't you?" Lennox asked.

Ouellette ignored him. Her shoulder and elbows and knees were still muddy and grass-stained from hitting the ground, and she was probably still inwardly vexed about that missing cufflink.

He slammed the door and took center stage under the stern and wounded portrait of Silas Musgrave. Ouellette stood off to one side. All eyes turned to him. He smiled.

"Patience Anne Musgrave was a wild child, the black sheep," he began. "She drank. She smoked. She ran around with boys. She was unworthy of the ancient Musgrave family name. She may have been a thorn in your side, Agatha, but she was her Uncle Charles's favorite. He made her the backup beneficiary in his will—if anything happened to his old Harvard roommate and best man at his wedding, the money all went to Patience when she turned twenty-one. And that gave you ideas, Agatha. You decided you had to kill him.

"Things only got worse when Patience came home one day and told you one of the local boys had gotten her pregnant. That was the last straw. You had her declared mentally incompetent, committed her to Danvers State, and you became her legal guardian. She had her baby, and named him Charles after her favorite uncle. And you put him right the hell up for adoption—you couldn't get rid of him fast enough, and Patience had no say in what happened. With Patience and her son squared away, and George Linnell run over and killed, you were now in charge of just over three-quarters of a million dollars, Agatha.

"But… then there was Laura. Thick as thieves, from what I hear. All excited that big sister Patience was going to have a baby and she was going to be Auntie Laura. She had no idea what was really going on, no idea about all your scheming. She just knew there was a baby on the way and she couldn't wait for her big sister to come home from the hospital with that little bundle of joy. And while she was waiting, she did Patience a favor. Nobody else had done it yet, you must have all forgotten, right? So thirteen-year-old Laura figured she'd take care of it."

Lennox moved over to the table, where the Bible still lay. He gently opened it to the first page. There, in many different hands and many different inks, was the Musgrave family tree, stretching back centuries, back to England, generation upon generation of births, deaths, and marriages recorded for all time. Lennox ran a finger down the page to where the present generation was listed.

"*Patience Anne Musgrave, b. March 11, 1951,*" was written in a firm angular hand, with a fountain pen. Probably written there by her father, Phillip.

Next to Patience's name, in a round, adolescent cursive, written with a blue ballpoint, was "*and Chris Maitland*."

Below those names, in the same looping script, was "*Charles Christopher Maitland, b. July 8, 1967*."

"You hit the roof when you found about this, didn't you, Agatha?" She would not return his gaze. "You were trying to hush all this up, and now she writes it all down in the family Bible, and it would always be there, *forever*. She needs to be punished, right? Can't send two daughters to Danvers, people would start to talk. So you just made her miserable, maybe even knocked her around a little. Years later, you tried to make it up to her by sending her off to Barnard… with Patience's money, by the way.

"And then when you ran Maitland out of town—"

Agatha and Christopher Maitland glowered at one another from opposite sides of the room. Lennox saw it, and saw something between them. Some old, shared secret.

"You swore I'd never see you again after that day," Agatha said accusingly.

"What day?" Lennox asked, looking back and forth between the two of them. "The day… the day he left Salem. He came here… oh, my God. Your self-made man story, that two thousand dollars… you didn't make that painting garages. You got it from Agatha. What did you do, show up and threaten to expose her if she didn't buy you off?"

Silence and angry faces.

"Maitland," Lennox went on, incredulously. "That money she gave you that day—that was *Patience's money*. You realize that, right? My God… you ended up stealing from her too, you sick bastard."

It took him a minute to catch his breath and continue.

"Fifty years later, Patience's son, all grown up, appears on your doorstep, big as life. Maybe he knows what you did to his mother, maybe he's here to expose you. Maybe he's here looking for his inheritance, the money you stole from his mother, the money that probably should be his. And you panicked. So you gave him a story.

We need to talk to the family lawyer, draw up some papers, make some arrangements for you. We can straighten it all out tomorrow over tea. See you then. And as soon as he's out the door, you're planning to kill him. It's the only solution you can see, Agatha.

"Because the money is gone now, isn't it? Pissed away over the years. Sending Laura off to Barnard was probably the end of it. So if he wants his inheritance, there isn't one. Yeah, this is big, big trouble."

Lennox's face was bright red, and he spoke with a kind of indignation that Ouellette had not seen in him for a long time. Not since before the shooting. It was strangely reassuring.

"He comes back the next day. You show him the family Bible—see, you're right here, you're my long-lost grandson, our long-lost nephew. Welcome home. One lump or two?

"And you're ready for him. You formulated your plan while he was out later that day with Laura, visiting Patience's grave."

He could see it in his mind as he said it. He could imagine Agatha smiling her vicious yellow smile, pouring tea and offering a buttery scone as Benedict came up from behind with the leather cord. Throwing it over Charles's head, pulling hard, leather biting into flesh. Charles's face turning a nasty purple, Laura screaming to stop, as Charles turned, slipped out. Whirling, he sank a solid punch to Benedict's face...

"Now all this time, we've been looking at you for this, Benny. You're the one with the history of violence. Agatha's an invalid, doesn't get up out of that chair, and I always knew Laura couldn't have had a hand in this. So all along, I was convinced it was you. But I was wrong.

"Because it was *you*, Agatha."

The old woman's eyes came up to meet his. Her lips curled in a cruel little half-smile.

Agatha was not Louisa Prescott; she was a throwback to those early settlers who had built Salem, had carved a village out of that howling wilderness. People with strong backs and knotted hands and hard eyes. She wasn't ever going to confess to a damned thing.

"You can get up out of that chair, you just don't. Because that's the kind of manipulative old bitch you are. You can get up out of that chair—if you have a good reason. You just showed us all that when you saw Maitland. When Charles—when your *grandson*—got away from Benedict suddenly, you had a good reason. You grabbed that candlestick and you swung—three, four, five times, even after he went down. Until he was dead.

"But… now you had a whole new set of problems. You had to get rid of the body, deal with the evidence, clean up the crime scene, and hope to God you didn't miss anything. Scalp wounds bleed like hell, and beating him over the head again and again while he writhed around on the floor… blood went everywhere, didn't it? Now the rug caught most of it, and you were able to clean up whatever didn't land on the rug where he was standing. But the rug didn't catch all of it."

He turned back to the big Bible on the table. Drops of dark blood were sprayed across the page, across the Musgrave family tree. How oddly fitting, he thought.

"The Bible was still out, still open, and caught some of the spatter. Now this, this is a serious problem. This is a piece of evidence you can't get rid of. This is the family Bible, family heirloom passed down the generations. It's too valuable in too many ways to just get rid of. So you need to hide it, and you do, deep down in old Silas's hidden cellars, where he used to get up to God-only-knows what. But you have to have a Bible on the shelf—everyone in town knows that Cotton Mather himself read from the Musgrave family Bible out there on Gallows Hill. So you dig out one from the collection of old Dr. John Musgrave, the collector from the 1890s. You put one of his on the shelf and stash the rest down in the cellar so we wouldn't find more than one Bible in the house and start to wonder.

"The fact that his name is now Mather is a hell of a weird coincidence, but it gives you an idea. Finding a body out at Gallows Hill—hanging at Gallows Hill, with pentagrams on his palms—that would have us asking all the wrong questions and make us go chasing after nothing, look for a witch connection, some occult angle. If we ever identified the body, ever found the name Paul Mather, that'd just be even more confusing.

"But… it never read like an occult crime to me. Even before we found that cross under his shirt, I had my doubts. Because you left the body at the foot of the hill. To the true believers in town, it's the top of the hill that's the important site. If it was some kind of an occult crime, the rain wouldn't stop a murderer from getting the body to the summit.

"So Benedict, you're the one who dumps the body, and Laura is told to get rid of the car. Easy enough—she drives it over to Beverly and leaves it there. You pick her up and bring her home. But she's completely freaked out by everything that's happened, and she's on the verge of a breakdown. She's on autopilot. She leaves the car, but she still has the key in one hand. Probably didn't even realize it.

"For a few days, it looks like you might have actually gotten away with it. The newspapers cover the story, and say the police are making no progress, thank you very much. The Salem police don't handle murders, they can't possibly know what they're doing. All you have to do is sit tight, deny everything, and let the case go cold. All we had was suspicion and supposition anyway."

He turned back to Benedict for a moment.

"But you wanted to destroy the Bible. After you cleaned up, the Bible was the only really damning evidence left. Better to get rid of that once and for all, right? But Agatha wouldn't allow it. Can't destroy the family Bible, even if it is a key piece of evidence in a homicide investigation.

"You argued. It got out of hand and Laura called 911—she thought you were going to hit your mother. You didn't know what to do. You needed advice. You did what everybody in town does sooner or later—you got your tarot cards read. I don't know what Symboline told you, and I don't really care. Doesn't make any difference. Mommy dearest put her foot down. That Bible wasn't going anywhere. Trouble in paradise. You went to stay out in the carriage house until this all blew over.

"Laura was having her own problems. She was an accessory to the murder of her own nephew. Talk about your quiet desperation. But she had some breathing room—she'd been able to take a few steps away from the family. She'd been to college in New York, she'd gotten married and moved out of the family home. She wasn't completely under your thumb, Agatha, not like Benedict. She had some sort of chance. And she had to do something about all of this, so she reached out to me. But… she couldn't break with the family completely. She sent me an anonymous note, saying that Charles had indeed been here, and that all the evidence we were looking for was in the family Bible. And so it is.

"If she had come to us, the lawyers would have put her in front of the grand jury and we would have arrested you all on her testimony. But an anonymous note… that's not considered a reliable source of information. We came back with search warrants and still didn't really move things forward very far."

He paused for a moment.

"And then poor Laura couldn't take it anymore," he went on in a low voice. "She was too conflicted, and she tried to kill herself."

And she might never wake up.

"By now, all of this had hit the news, and you heard about it," he turned to Christopher Maitland. "You'd made good since leaving Salem with your blood money. Successful businessman, well-known philanthropist, about to run for office. You couldn't let it get out that you'd fathered a child with your underage girlfriend when you were seventeen. You knew Laura had put you down in the family Bible as the father of Patience's child—she told you about it, didn't she, all those years ago? People might not accept that as proof, but it would be embarrassing and you would have a hell of a lot of explaining to do and that could very well cost you an election. You couldn't let this get out. Not after you fought so hard to save your career—you might not survive a second hit. You didn't know about the blood spatter, you couldn't have, you just knew your name was in that Bible, and you were scared to death that we'd find it.

"So you sent him to steal it," Lennox gestured toward Scully, huddled in the far corner. "But he got caught. And you're the one who sent the lawyer to bail him out—you've done work for Essex Partners, haven't you? Did they owe you a favor? Your thug gets caught, you still don't have the Bible, and now you're getting even more nervous. Now you're getting desperate.

"So you sounded us out. You wanted us to think you were a father concerned about his long-lost son, but you were trying to figure out how much we knew. And you reasoned that if we didn't know who you were, then we hadn't found the Bible yet. You had another chance to get your hands on it before we did. So you sent Scully in again."

Lennox turned to Scully.

"This isn't your first run-in with the law," he said. "You know things go a lot easier when you help the nice policeman."

"My boss works for him, for Maitland, owes him a favor," Scully said sullenly. "So… I was supposed to steal the Bible and hand it over at the Common. The family didn't want to give it up at first, but once I shot the eyes outta that painting, they got with the program. The big guy," he nodded toward Benedict, "he went down into that cellar and got it. But I could tell he wanted to kick my ass."

"So Benny came after you—he had one last chance to destroy that Bible but… too slow, Benny. Story of your life, eh?"

He laughed a dry, exhausted laugh that shook his shoulders. He hated these people, he realized. He really did. They had tormented him, haunted him for weeks, pinching him and pricking him, and damn near giving him fits. Yes, he hated these people. Agatha, Benedict, Maitland, Scully. Every damn one of them.

"So, I look around the room here and I see murder, conspiracy to commit murder, obstruction of justice, evidence tampering, breaking and entering, and that's just for starters…" He shook his head sadly. "God, Michelle and I will be filling out paperwork on all of you for the next month, but I for one could not be happier."

Chapter XXIV

NOVEMBER FIRST WAS THE QUIETEST DAY of the year in Salem. The only sound to be heard was tourists packing up and leaving as locals came blinking out into the morning sunlight, wondering what had hit them. Business owners slept in; there would be plenty of time to count up all the money later. Visitors may have planned and waited all year for that last night of October, but residents planned and waited for the first morning of November even more.

Lennox and Ouellette were at the station by noon, and leftover Halloween candy and empty wrappers were scattered across various desks in the bullpen. With Halloween being what it was in Salem, it was extraordinary that there was leftover candy to be found anywhere in town.

"How did Roland do last night?" Lennox asked.

"He had a good time. He was a pirate. My sister took him. Again. I always miss Halloween with him…"

She gave that tight smile, and despite her cool exterior, her infamous deadpan, Lennox caught just a flicker of the woman beneath it, the wistful mother disappointed that she had missed taking her son trick-or-treating.

"Next year," Lennox said. "Next year, I'll make sergeant and take the overnight shift, and you can go trick-or-treating, okay?"

Her smile loosened and warmed. "Okay. Thanks."

"Nicely done, detectives," Winters said, coming into the bullpen with coffee and doughnuts, his annual November First tradition for the detectives under his command. "Congratulations everyone."

"Thank you, sir," Ouellette nodded. "Couldn't have done it without Andrew."

Lennox gave what he hoped was a modest grin.

"Sergeant Dworaczyk was also very helpful," she said, gesturing over to where he sat reading the front page coverage of the case. The *Advertiser* ran the headline *Murder Case Closed!* while the *Argus* went with *Gallows Hill Murder Solved!* The *Advertiser* had a full-color photo of the detectives dragging the grim-faced Benedict and Maitland from the family mansion, with the velvet-cloaked Harker bringing up the rear, pushing the handcuffed Agatha along in her antiquated wheelchair. Dworaczyk seemed vexed that he was mentioned nowhere in either paper.

"Good job, all of you," Winters said, handing out cups of coffee.

Lennox rose stiffly from his desk. He'd gotten almost no sleep and had spent most of the day hunched over his desk filling out paperwork on the case. He handed a loose stack of papers over to the Lieutenant.

"There will be more," he promised. "Right now, I have to stretch my legs."

"Take your time, detective."

He wandered down the corridor to where the tired Johnson sat and held a massive styrofoam cup with both hands. She'd been at the state crime lab with a team of forensics experts all night, going over the Bible.

"We lifted plenty of blood samples from the page," she smiled. "Good news—it's Charles Musgrave's blood."

"Good news indeed," he smiled back, realizing that cops regarded the most gruesome things as good news. "So... I was wondering. To completely change the subject, does that Surrealists offer still stand? The case is closed, so I was wondering..."

"The offer still stands," she said. She blushed slightly. "Wednesday at seven. Rockafellas after?"

"Of course," he flushed. "All right then... Johnson."

"Amy," she corrected. "But everybody calls me A. J."

"All right then, A. J. Wednesday at seven it is."

He stopped to catch his breath out in the parking lot, inhaling deeply, letting the cool Autumn air fill his lungs, and realizing he didn't want a cigarette at all.

The curtains of the hospital room were drawn and the monitors glowed eerily in the gloom. Something was beeping regularly somewhere, and while it wasn't quite as utterly unnerving as it had been on his previous visits to Laura's bedside, Lennox still found the tinny beeps disconcerting.

Laura Musgrave Gagnon had lain unconscious for three days, and had never been far from his mind. He'd come here as often as he could, sitting in the room, waiting, hoping. A few times, he realized he was praying. The legal action her husband and his lawyers—plural—were threatening didn't bother him nearly so much as the thought that because of him, the woman in the bed across the room might never wake up.

And then she did.

Laura convulsed and gasped for air, like a swimmer surfacing from too deep a dive. She coughed and hacked and blinked. And she slowly, painfully sat up, staring at the tubes in her arms, the plastic hospital tag around one pale wrist.

"Where am I?" she croaked.

"You're in the hospital," Lennox said. "North Shore Medical."

"Detective Lennox?"

"Yes," he said, buzzing for the nurse. He hit the button over and over. "Just try to stay still. How do you feel?"

"I don't… I don't know yet."

"Just try to take it easy."

"My family… the… murder investigation…" she whispered.

"That's over for now. Don't worry about it. Don't worry about anything right now."

He didn't tell her about the long talk he and Ouellette had had with the Attorney General, how they recommended Laura be charged with disposing of stolen property, and not be included in the murder and conspiracy charges pending against Agatha and Benedict. She was a witness, not a suspect. In her own scared way, she had reached out to him, tried to help. She should be spared. She was a brand, he thought, plucked from the burning.

At the trial, months later, Laura would describe the events of that awful night a few weeks before Halloween, the night her nephew Charles was murdered in the family home. She would also describe him, Charles, the long-lost Musgrave heir, the soft-spoken man with shy eyes and awkward gestures, speaking about the death of his wife in a flat Midwest twang. He'd known almost nothing of the stolen inheritance, she would tell the jury, and didn't even care. He was a man who had come searching for his family, and had found them, and he was happy. He was a decent man, Laura would say. He was truly Patience's son, the kind who would give a retarded kid his red jello.

"I'll have the nurse call your husband," Lennox said. "He can be here in a few minutes... I won't stay, though."

"Why not?"

"I'm not his favorite person right now. He's kind of... suing me, and the department." He shrugged. "He thinks you tried to kill yourself because of me, that I drove you to it."

"It wasn't you, detective."

"Andrew."

"It wasn't you, Andrew. I just couldn't take what was happening. I'll talk to Neil; I'll have him drop it."

"I'll ask the nurse to call him," Lennox nodded. "I'm sure he'll be glad to see you."

He made his way down the hospital corridor and paused for a moment by the nurses' station. A harried woman looked up from the desk.

"Yes?"

"I, um, found this on the floor down the corridor..." he said, fishing his last pack of Xanax from a coat pocket. "Someone must have dropped it, I guess."

The nurse took the pills and squinted at them.

"That Xanax?" she muttered.

"I wouldn't know," Lennox shrugged.

"I'll take care of it." She tossed the pack aside.

"Great. Thanks."

The sun was setting behind Gallows Hill as he arrived, crowning it in fire. Somehow, even the water tank looked regal silhouetted against the sun. Gray shadows crept out over the park.

The woman in white appeared as the sun sank lower and lower. She came over to stand next to him, next to the piles of dry flowers and blobs of melted candles. Her hands were empty.

"I saw the news," she said quietly. "It's over?"

Lennox nodded. "It's over."

"He can rest?"

"I think so."

"Good."

"No candle?" he asked.

"I don't need to light candles for him anymore," the strange woman replied. "Because of you. Thank you."

His cell phone beeped as the woman walked away.

"Detective Lennox?" asked a half-familiar voice. "Sergeant Michaelson, Danvers PD. We found Danny Dateline for you."

"You did?" Lennox laughed.

"Yeah. He was laying low, but we picked him up. The only problem you might have is that his parents showed up, and they might not be too happy about letting you talk to him."

"Yeah, well… it's not really a problem. We don't need him."

"You're sure?"

"I haven't been sure of anything in a long time, but I'm pretty sure about this. Thanks, Sergeant."

"Yeah, sure."

He hung up.

Winter was still weeks away, but there was a chill in the air, a change. Lennox didn't think it was just the season. The pagans in town said that the Great Wheel of the Year had turned, and a new year stretched out before them, a blank page. Maybe they were right. He hoped they were.

The setting sun lit the old city with reds and golds, this old old *old* city that neither could nor would get out from under the weight of its own history, this city he had memorized street by street, every corner haunted by some witch, some Puritan, some ghost. A city no one ever left. A city that he had slowly and strangely fallen in love with.

Lennox walked back to his apartment in the old jail. Tomorrow morning, police work would begin again, and he would drink coffee, fill out paperwork, and wait for the phone to ring.

From the author

YOU DON'T WRITE A BOOK ON YOUR OWN. At least I don't. The following splendid people were all of assistance in tangible or ineffable ways. Many thanks to them. I'm not crying, there's something in my eye.

My wife, Judith Reilly, who puts up with a lot. And I do mean a lot.

Susanne Bohne-Bencivenga read early drafts and offered much-needed feedback and encouragement.

Daniel Ciora, attorney at law, for help with some of the legal mumbo-jumbo.

Jeanette Coleman-Hall wrecked some antique silver for me, just to see what would happen.

Damien Cote and Vincent Courteau taught me to swear like a Quebecois; merci beaucoup.

Paul diFilippo leads by example and continues to inspire. I want to be just like him when I grow up.

Greg Easton answered one question after another about the US Coast Guard; thanks for your time and patience.

Tony Gangi took time out from a busy schedule of hammering nails up his nose and snapping mousetraps on his tongue to offer thorough and helpful feedback

Walter Greatshell very kindly read an early draft and offered feedback and encouragement; thanks, man.

Captain Thomas Griffin of the Salem Police Department's Criminal Investigation Division was very generous with his time and patience, answering oddball questions.

Sara J. Henry read an early draft and offered much-needed advice and encouragement.

David Higgins was very generous with his time and expertise; unfortunately, the scenes for which he gave me the benefit of his insight were eventually dropped in re-writes. Thanks anyway, Dave!

Jill Jann, best friend and proud owner of my favorite laugh ever, for introducing me to John Teehan in the first place and sending me in his direction again all these years later.

Amber Kelly read a draft one line at a time, on her phone. She offered feedback and encouragement, but more importantly, she read the damn thing one line at a time on her phone. Amber's a trouper. Thanks, dollface.

Lee Lofland answered obscure questions about police procedure.

Dr. D. P. Lyle answered questions about blood and Luminol, for which he earns my sanguinary, glowing thanks.

Tania Montenegro Rocha gave me the inside scoop on how things really work in hotels.

Susan O'Connell told me all about quitting smoking.

Danielle Oliveira Gelehrter helped me say things in Portuguese.

Paul Ramsay read, critiqued, and coached me through this, being generous and supportive all the way. Thanks, man.

Sgt. David Reilly, NYPD, the brother-in-law, was very generous and quite tolerant in answering endless, naïve (and probably endlessly naïve) questions about cop stuff.

Rick Sardinha is another helpful soul who offered medical insight to… scenes which were eventually cut.

John Teehan at Merry Blacksmith Press took a chance on a first-timer.

Elizabeth Wayland-Seal offered feedback, encouragement, and a laser-like eye for typos and inconsistencies, of which there were many. Can't thank you enough.

Any of you, really.

Visit www.roryobrienbooks.com

CPSIA information can be obtained at www.ICGtesting.com
Printed in the USA
LVOW12s2240010714

392627LV00010B/202/P